FINDING LOVE IN APARTMENT 2C

Samantha Baca

Contents

<u>One</u>

I stared at the blank screen in front of me as my fingers impatiently tapped against the keyboard. I was halfway through the rewrites for my manuscript and my editor confirmed that I needed to add in a steamy sex scene if I wanted to call this book a romance. The handful of options I had tossed her way were quickly returned to me with a reminder that my book was already written, leading up to a super-steamy love scene, so I needed to deliver. Apparently, I had no idea what was considered steamy sex anymore.

I pushed away from the computer and laid my head against the cool leather of my office chair as I closed my eyes and tried to forget about the fact that the fictional characters I had created were about to have more sex this weekend than I would have all year. This wasn't my first book, nor was it my first time writing a sex scene, yet I struggled with them every single time I had to write one. They all ended up being the same, no matter how hard I tried. And they were all boring and predictable according to my editor. *Hailey, it's too vanilla* she claimed before asking me to push myself to think sexy thoughts and try again.

Maybe if I had been one of those girls who was less focused on good grades in high school and more focused on boys, I would have a lot more to write about. There was nothing sexy about my 4.0 GPA. Guys weren't ready to take me to bed because I memorized the periodic table. My knowledge of the Cold War wasn't a huge turn on either. Those weren't the things that guys lusted after.

I glanced down at the clock on my computer screen and groaned when I saw that it was already after nine. I had been trying to write this damn scene for over two hours and I was still staring at the same blank page I had started with. Irritated, I got up and walked over to the fridge, opening the door to the freezer side to allow the cold air to cool me off.

It was mid-August and the summers in Arizona were brutal. Add on a random heatwave and my small two-bedroom apartment easily became a hot box that became impossible to cool down. Even though I was born and raised here, I was far from tolerant of the heat and should have moved somewhere cooler the moment that I graduated.

I reached into the ice bin and pulled out an ice cube, desperate for something to cool me off. I popped it in my mouth and was about to refill my glass with ice water when an idea hit me. Quickly, I pulled off my tank top and stood in front of the open freezer door wearing cutoff shorts and a bra as I grabbed another ice cube and slowly ran it across my shoulder before trailing it across my clavicle. I could feel the ice melting as the water dripped down my chest, my eyes closing as I tried to picture myself being turned on by it like the girls in the movies were.

Slowly I pushed it across to the other side of my body and ran it in circles as it continued to melt quickly beneath my fingers. I shut my eyes tighter, trying to force the sexy thoughts into my mind. A few seconds later I grunted as I tossed the small piece of ice that was left into the sink and grabbed a towel to dry myself off with. I was no cooler, not at all turned on, and now my bra was wet which just made me feel sticky. I rolled my eyes as I unhooked my bra in the back and tossed it on the couch as I put my tank top back on. It was stupid to think that ice could ever turn anyone on.

I filled my glass with ice and was about to press the button on the fridge to switch it to water when I heard a noise through the wall from the other apartment. I stood still and tilted my head toward the wall as I tried to listen. The sound wasn't clear, but it definitely sounded like moaning. Just my luck, I sighed and started filling my glass with water as I heard a thump against the wall. Followed by another. Soon there was a very continuous pattern and I knew my very promiscuous, very attractive neighbor was having sex. When wasn't he? He hadn't lived there long, but in the few months he had been there he had a different woman with him every time I saw him.

As I was about to walk back to my desk and stare at the blank page, another thought snuck into my mind and I found myself grabbing a notepad and pen from the counter before I quickly rushed off to stand by the wall as I listened. I tried to get as close as I could get, taking a few steps in each direction until I found the perfect spot where I could hear everything clearer. My hand worked quickly as I tried to write down as many juicy details as I could before it was over.

Once they were done there was a collective sigh as I tossed my notepad and pen down and massaged my hand which had cramped up from the intense writing sprint. I heard voices as they walked towards the door, more muffled the further they walked away. A few seconds later I heard the door open then close, knowing that his booty call was on her way. I picked myself up off the floor by the couch and made my way back to my desk to write the sex scene that had come so easily to me after that.

It was after ten by the time I wrapped up the chapter I had been working on. I still had a handful of other sex scenes to work through that needed my attention, but they would have to wait until another burst of creativity hit me. There were still two weeks left before my deadline, which gave me a very small window to work through wrapping everything up and getting the final manuscript to my editor.

It had felt weird to actively listen to my neighbor have sex through the thin wall tonight, then turn around and write about it. Part of me was ashamed listening in when I should have walked away but the other part of me was relieved that it had helped me get what I needed for my book. Their dialogue, from what I could hear, was dirty and flowed so easily that I was almost able to use it verbatim. I changed a few things to tone it down some because, dear Lord, it got pretty filthy, but for the most part it gave me the edge I was needing.

I made sure for the hundredth time to save my file before shutting down my computer. It was late and my body was sore from sitting for so long. I debated on whether to finish cleaning up the kitchen tonight or leave it until the morning. I blew out a heavy sigh when I knew that my Type A personality wasn't going to wait until the morning. As quickly as I could, I cleaned up the mess from dinner, tossing the takeout boxes in the trash and wiping down the counters. The trash was overly full and I didn't want to deal with it tonight, but I also didn't want to deal with the smell that would surely linger in the room from the empty food containers.

I quickly pulled my curly, dark auburn brown hair up into a messy ponytail and grabbed the trash bag to take it downstairs to the dumpster. I made my way back up the stairs, not paying attention to anything other than the naughty thoughts that were still racing through my mind when I felt a hard jolt as my body crashed into a hard, warm body. My cheeks flushed as I felt his hand grab onto my hip, steadying me in place as we stood facing each other. It felt like being in a movie, his perfectly toned chest glistening in the dim light that hung above us. I swallowed hard as I tried to look away and not focus on the piece of sex-on-a-stick that stood in front of me. Even though I hadn't watched him have sex, I felt so embarrassed that he might know that I had been listening. I looked down and saw a trash bag in his hand and wondered why everyone felt the need to take their trash out at this hour on a Saturday night. Didn't we have anything better to do?

"Hey." His voice was low and for a moment I wondered if he was actually talking to me. I don't think we had said one word to each other since he moved in other than a few head nods here and there, the acknowledgment of another human in our presence.

I swallowed hard as my eyes slowly moved up to meet his, the sapphire blue color taking my breath away. I had only seen him around a handful of times but never this close. Never close enough to notice the natural blonde highlights that were weaved throughout his hair, evidence of plenty of time spent outside in the sun. I licked my lips and tilted my head, replaying the dirty things I had heard him say earlier.

"Are you okay?" he asked as he dropped his hand from my waist and leaned against the rail, setting the trash bag down beside him. I quickly blinked my eyes several times trying to force myself out of the dirty daze I was in.

"Yeah, I'm sorry." I made eye contact with him and tried to smile. Big mistake. "I'm Hailey, I live next door. You're super hot tonight."

His eyes went wide with amusement as my hand flew to my mouth in embarrassment. His smile spanned across his face showcasing a mouth full of perfectly straight, white teeth, clearly enjoying this moment of utter humiliation for me.

"I mean, IT'S super hot tonight. Not you." I shook my head and looked away before he could see the heat in my cheeks from blushing.

"So you don't think I'm hot?" His tone was playful, the words oozing right out of him as easily as the dirty words I heard coming from him not that long ago. I kept looking off into the distance, avoiding eye contact as much as I could.

"Of course I do," I whispered, my mouth suddenly dry as cotton. "I mean, I don't know? Do you think you are?" I bit down on my tongue to try to keep myself from saying anything else. This was so embarrassing. I needed to just say goodnight and go inside and pray that I never saw him again.

"I don't know if I would say hot... good looking, maybe. I mean, the women don't seem to complain." He winked as he said it as if we shared some secret I didn't know about. I swallowed hard as the heat continued to prickle my skin, sweat beads lining my hairline as I worried that he knew what I had done.

I could feel him pin me with a look, holding me in place as I squirmed under his bolstering smirk.

"Yeah, so I've heard," I mumbled before my eyes shot up to look at him, my face turning beet red again, as I watched another smile pull at the corners of his mouth. He arched an eyebrow as he crossed his arms over his bare chest and said nothing.

"I really should be going," I said as I tried to take the last few steps past him to get to my apartment. My head whipped around to look at him when I felt warm fingers gently wrap around my arm, holding me in place.

"What exactly have you heard?" He chewed his bottom lip as he watched me, waiting for an answer.

"Nothing. I um... yeah, nothing." I crossed my arms over my chest, mimicking him when I suddenly remembered that I never got around to putting my bra back on. I glanced down to make sure nothing was showing while trying to be as discreet as possible. I watched as his eyes slowly followed mine down my body, my arms suddenly drawing his attention to my bare chest.

"I better get going, have a good night." I looked down and watched where I stepped as I navigated past the trash bag and made my way to my apartment. I could hear him chuckle as he picked up the trash bag and went downstairs. Once inside, I closed and locked the door behind me. I leaned against it and slid down, holding my head in my hands as I replayed our conversation. If I thought it was going to be hard looking at him after hearing him have sex, our brief conversation just confirmed that it would be damn near impossible to ever be around him again.

Two

The days flew by as I struggled with staring at a blank screen, again, while avoiding my neighbor. How was it even fair that he was that incredibly good looking? I had no idea what he did for a living, but I would be surprised if model or sex god wasn't on his resume. I knew the intimate details of his life, like how he had absolutely zero body hair on his impeccable body and got up early every morning to work out before leaving at 7:37 for work, but yet I didn't even know his name.

By Tuesday morning, I had also avoided a call from my editor for the third time since Sunday. I sent her the updated sex scene that I wrote Saturday night to make sure I was on the right path and suddenly she had too many questions about how I came up with the details for it. Needless to say, I wasn't in the mood to confess to her that I had eavesdropped on my gorgeous next-door neighbor as he had sex with some random girl, got myself so hot and bothered that I was able to write about it before rushing off to my bedroom to relieve the tension he had inadvertently created. See what I mean? Sex god. Who else can turn women on without even trying??

I needed to come up with a better explanation for the super sexy scene that I had written, but better yet, I needed to find a way to create another one. My mind was drawing blanks left and right, nothing sexy or different than what I usually write. The day dragged on and before I knew it, I was staring at an empty Chinese food container as I twirled the chopsticks around praying the damn thing would just write itself. I heard a chime and glanced down to see another text from my best friend, Amanda, checking to make sure I was still alive. She knew me well enough to know not to bother with calling when I was facing a deadline.

I got up to throw my trash away and stretch my legs, a much-needed break after sitting at my desk for hours. As I cleaned up my mess and washed my hands, I heard the distinct sound of the sex god's door open and close, voices softly filtered in through the wall. I dried my hands quickly and tossed the towel on the counter as I walked over to the wall and pressed my ear next to it to try to hear who he was with tonight.

A few minutes later, the voices started to fade away before they were replaced with moaning. I almost giggled out loud as I thought about how this guy didn't waste any time. Either he was incredibly skilled, and these women were just willing and ready to go the second they walked in, or maybe he was actually hiring women to come sleep with him. If they were being paid by the hour that would explain the quick jumpstart to their activities.

I rolled my eyes and shook my head knowing damn well that a guy like that wasn't paying for sex. I mean, I would pay him for sex but that didn't mean that he was as pathetic as I was at the moment. The moaning grew louder, almost like they were coming closer. I took a cautious step back, feeling awkward again for listening but finding it impossible to walk away. I heard a loud thump as I noticed the framed picture on the wall above the couch shake, my eyes going wide when I realized that they were having sex on the other side of the wall.

The rhythmic banging against the wall confirmed that he indeed had her pinned to the wall as he plowed into her. Not that I had to leave it to my imagination to figure out what position they were in, his filthy mouth explicitly directed her to wrap her legs around him so he could fuck her pussy harder. His words, not mine.

I let out a shaky breath, frustrated with myself for once again failing to walk away when I knew they were having sex, but also for allowing myself to get so turned on by it. Reluctantly I made my way over to the couch and sat down, leaning into the cushion as I tilted my head toward their voices. I closed my eyes as I focused on the sounds behind me. The consistent thud against the wall. The way she moaned, louder as she got closer. His deep grunts as he moved quicker and harder. There wasn't much dialogue this time, just two people moaning their way through what sounded like a very intense build-up.

My fingers trailed down my neck and over my chest, playing with the idea of touching myself as I listened. Within seconds I was leaning back against a pillow, my fingers deep inside of me, working in the same fast rhythm as I brought myself to climax simultaneously with their cries of ecstasy. I took a deep breath and pulled my hand away, the shame of what I had done quickly replacing the relief I had mere seconds before.

What in the world was wrong with me? I wasn't this person. I was the author who made up stories and allowed her creativity to flow in every word before paying a professional to twist them into something that people would want to buy. I wasn't the girl who sat around and listened to other people have sex while getting myself off. Was I?

I blew out a breath, forcing a stray curl out of my eyes as I got up and made my way to the bathroom. Embarrassment continued to take its hold on me, eating away at how I could have gotten to this point in my life. Maybe I need to make more friends and get out of the house more? Perhaps I needed to try dating again? Something needed to change, and I needed it to happen soon before I got too obsessed with this new hobby.

My fingers itched to sit down and write the sex scene that was rushing through my head. Instead, I forced myself to brush my teeth and get in bed, ignoring the fact that my deadline was a week and a half away and I really needed to write this. Part of me justified that I needed to write it tomorrow, with a clear mind, but the other part of me knew that this wasn't something that I could keep up much longer. I couldn't stake my career on having a constant supply of fresh sex scenes from the sex god next door to motivate me. What if he moved?

I shook my head at the thought and climbed under the covers, kicking them off as quickly as I had pulled them on. It was more out of habit than anything given that it was still 100 degrees outside and far from cold. I rolled onto my side and tried to clear my mind but the only thing I could think about was how arousing tonight had been. I hadn't felt that turned on or alive in… ever? And to think that I wasn't even the one making love to him. Then it hit me- what if I never found someone who would make me feel this way? What if I was destined to be alone, relying on the experiences of others to make me feel fulfilled. I closed my eyes and tried to push the depressing thoughts out of my head as I continued to doubt that a life like that would ever exist for me.

<u>Three</u>

The sun peeked around the curtains, casting a warm yellow glow on the beige-colored walls. I groaned as I looked over and glanced at the clock on the nightstand beside my bed, knowing that it was time to get up. I slid my legs over the bed and stretched, trying to get some blood flowing through my body to wake me up. The sun was shining. The birds were chirping. And it was Wednesday which meant the sex scenes should come easy to me today since it was hump day after all.

I rolled my eyes at the cheesy one-liner before debating on whether to write it down to use later in another book. Desperation had to be pretty strong if I was actually considering it. I made my way into the bathroom, showered, and threw my wet, curly hair up into a tight ponytail on top of my head. I needed to crack the whip today and make some serious progress or I wasn't going to be able to make my deadline.

The sound of coffee brewing was music to my ears as I turned on my computer and set everything up that I needed. Notepad- check. Pens- check. Water bottle filled with ice water- check. Music turned on- check. I bounced around the room, tidying up a few things and fluffing the pillows on the couch as the music filled the air around me. It was an upbeat playlist with songs that were guaranteed to make me want to get up and dance. Either I was going to kick some ass and get these sex scenes done today, or I was going to get one hell of a workout. I wasn't sure which.

I was still bopping my head while filling my coffee cup when I heard a loud knock on my door. I pulled my brows together as I patted down my pockets to find my phone, turning the music down as I walked to the door to answer it. The music was quiet as I opened the door, expecting to see my elderly neighbor who on occasion would stop by to borrow something she had accidentally run out of. She was sweet as honey but hard of hearing which sometimes made it hard to talk to her before she would get frustrated and wander back to her apartment.

As the door swung open, I felt my jaw drop when I saw Mr. Sex God on the other side wearing a T-shirt and denim shorts instead of his usual business casual work attire. I tilted my head as my brain tried to figure out what to say. The idea that he had come to my apartment was too mind-boggling to let actual thoughts process.

"Are you okay?" He peered at me through squinted eyes as he waited for me to respond.

"Um, yeah. Sorry." I shook my head, trying to force out every arousing thought that was threatening to take over the conversation. "What's up?" I gripped the side of the door as I hid my body next to it, trying to disappear.

"I hate to sound like a crotchety old man, but would you mind keeping the music down a little? I'm working on a project from home today and desperately need to focus or I'm going to miss the deadline." He held his hands up in front of him, begging as he smiled warmly at me.

I felt my cheeks flush, embarrassed.

"Of course, I'm sorry," I stuttered, still struggling to form coherent thoughts while inhaling the scent of his body wash that was lingering in the air between us. "I don't usually have my music up loud, I was trying to get myself hyped up so I could meet my deadline too."

There was a curiosity in his eyes as he listened, his eyes slightly shifting behind me to take in my apartment as if that would give him some sort of idea as to what I was working on.

"Well, I hate to kill your motivation today, especially if you were in the zone. I can go work somewhere else if you need the loud music to focus," he offered as he pointed behind him toward a coffee shop across the street.

"No, it's okay. Really. I don't usually use music to focus so I don't even know that it would work. I'll figure something else out. Thanks." I smiled nervously, my palms sweating as I maintained my grip on the door.

"Okay," he sighed and shrugged his broad shoulders. "If you change your mind..." He raised his eyebrows as he turned to go back to his apartment. I smiled politely and nodded my head as I watched him smile and walk back into his apartment. A second later, the door clicked as it shut behind him and I let out the breath I had been holding. I closed the door and leaned against it, feeling completely rattled by our interaction, though brief as it was.

I allowed myself a few seconds to recover, my legs feeling weak from being so close to him. More-so from fighting the urge to climb his body like a cat climbing a tree. This interaction felt so much more intense than the one we had on Saturday night and I wondered if my body could sense how sexual of a person he was or if it was my brain punishing me for allowing myself to keep engaging in these absurd fantasies every night.

Any possible motivation I was hoping to have was quickly tossed out the window after he left. I grabbed my coffee off of the kitchen counter and set it down on my desk as I plopped down into the leather chair, hoping that sitting in front of the computer would be enough to put me in the right mindset to get this done.

Hours later I still had no new sex scenes and a handful of doodles on the notepad beside me. My stomach growled, reminding me that it was still hungry from a missed breakfast. Reluctantly, I got up, took my coffee cup to the sink, and opened the fridge to look for suitable lunch options.

I pulled out a loaf of bread along with some lunch meat and cheese to make a sandwich when I heard a knock outside. It was too faint to be my door, so I ignored it as I went back to laying more lunch meat on top of the slice of cheese. It was far from gourmet, but it would do. A few minutes later, I heard a door open followed by muffled voices, one of which was definitely female.

I put the meat and cheese back in the fridge and closed it. I picked up my sandwich and glanced at the clock on the stove to make sure I hadn't totally lost my mind and that it really was only 12:30 and not 8 p.m. His patterns for having a different girl come over every night had somehow become a routine for me which made this random visitor feel odd and out of place. Go away girl, it's not booty call time yet.

The voices were muffled so I tried my best to just ignore them as I sat on the couch and ate my sandwich. My mind wandered as I closed my eyes and tried to relax so this new brain fog would lift and allow me to do my job. I slowly chewed each bite, creating a sort of Zen-like atmosphere as I kept my eyes closed and focused on the silence around me. Only it wasn't silent anymore. There was the definitive sound of flirting happening right on the other side of the wall.

I grunted as I popped the last bite into my mouth and stood up, wiping my hands on the napkin before throwing it in the trash. I had to get work done but that wasn't going to happen any time soon, especially not with this new distraction. I walked to my desk and was about to sit down when a flirty laugh made its way through the walls. Lucky bitch, I thought, as jealousy reared its ugly head.

I could try to sit down and force the sex scenes along, pray for the best, and hope that I still had a job after this book tanked. Or I could give up and come back to it when things weren't so distracting. I toyed with the idea of sitting down and listening, convincing myself that it was merely research and not at all a creepy violation of the sex god's privacy.

A few minutes later I was sitting in the hallway between our apartments with a notepad and pen in hand as my stomach soured from what a terrible idea this was. I pulled my knees up towards me, giving myself a sturdy surface to write on. I leaned my head to the side, trying to make out what they were saying but it was still a little muffled. Definitely clearer than what I could hear inside through the wall, but still muffled. I quickly scooted over, getting closer to his door and leaning back to see if I could hear better.

Before I knew it, I was leaning against his door with my head turned to the side, my ear was pressed against it. So far this was the best position to hear everything clearly without actually being in the room with them. There was some general conversation, a few questions about the project, and the deadline before I heard the change in her tone. Suddenly it was dead silent. I was about to jump up and run back into my apartment before I got caught when I heard the first moan. So that's why it got quiet, I chuckled and held my hand over the paper, ready to start taking notes.

I had no idea if this was one of the same girls who had been by before or if it was a new girl, but they definitely went faster than he usually did the other times I had heard him. There was hardly any talking, just some quick dirty talk before he commanded her into new positions. I could feel the energy flowing through me as my hand flew across the paper, writing everything down as quickly as I could. I was so caught up in the moment that I hadn't heard them stop. My hand was still writing when I suddenly heard the door open, my back falling to the floor as I looked up at him with humiliation etched on my face.

His eyes went wide in surprise as he stepped to the side to avoid having me fall on him. The surprise quickly turned to amusement as I watched one eyebrow arch up in question as he took in the notepad and pen in my hand as I scurried to get up. I could hear water running in the bathroom and felt my face turn red as the thought of the woman he was having sex with just a few minutes ago was about to come out and catch me spying on them.

I stood nervously in front of him as I clutched the notepad to my chest and panicked as I tried to figure out what to say.

"I didn't expect to find you sitting in front of my apartment," he said as he nodded to where I had been a few seconds before. I swallowed hard as I studied him, shirtless with his arms folded over his chest.

"Sorry about that, I was just trying to get some work done," I lied as I looked away, small beads of sweat covering his chest. The guilt of knowing why they were there was making me anxious that he would know what I was doing.

"In front of my door? What kind of work were you doing?" He tilted his head, licking his lips before pulling the bottom one in between his teeth.

"Research?" My voice rose a full octave as I debated whether I should look as crazy as I was about to sound and just run back to my apartment and lock myself inside forever so I would never have to see him again.

"Research," he repeated. "What were you researching?" He stepped closer, invading my personal space, paralyzing me so I couldn't move.

"Um, it's research... about... birds?" I looked up, finding myself pulled in by the dark blue eyes that were now holding me in place.

"Birds." He nodded his head as he took this information in. "That's funny, I didn't realize that my apartment was such a hot spot for bird research. What exactly were you studying?"

It was as if he was the first boy to ever talk to me. My body and brain were definitely not on the same page as my body was saying- lean a little closer and lick that sweat off his chest, while my head was convincing me to talk about birds.

"Just you know, general stuff," I said, waving dismissively in the air between us. I felt my cheeks blush as I glanced down at the notepad that was still clutched to my chest, knowing that there was nothing as remotely innocent as a bird written on the pages where I had furiously scribbled down the details of his sexcapade.

As if sensing that I was lying, he looked down at the notepad and smirked. I felt my heart beat faster as I turned to walk away.

"Sorry for bothering you, I should-" As I turned to walk out of his apartment, I felt his arm reach out and grab the notepad. Mortified, I spun around and gasped when I saw his eyes light up once he saw what I had written down. A smile pulled across his face as he chewed his bottom lip before looking up at me knowingly. I felt the color drain from my face before I sprinted out of the room and back into my apartment, slamming the door closed behind me. I leaned against it and slowly slid to the floor praying that I could stay inside forever and never have to see him again.

Four

I paced back and forth behind my door, nervously chewing my fingernail as I tried to process what just happened. One second everything was fine- I was hanging out, minding my own business, then BAM I'm laying at his feet, looking up at this gorgeous specimen who now has the notepad with all of the dirty things I just listened to him do. Okay, so maybe I wasn't minding my own business and maybe this was karma sinking its teeth into my big, round ass.

My hands were shaking as I tried to come down from the adrenaline that shot through me when he took the notepad, forcing me to run away and never look back. I took a deep breath and slowly forced it out as I tried to fan the air in front of me to help cool me down. It felt likc it had been hours ago yet the clock on the stove confirmed that only two minutes had passed since I stormed in here and locked myself in. I struggled to pull another deep breath in and was just about to exhale when I heard a knock on the door. I froze in place, holding my breath as I stared at the door. I cinched my eyes shut as I silently begged for it to be my elderly neighbor, Ms. O'Connell. A few seconds later I heard another knock followed by a deep voice.

"I know you're in there, I heard the door slam after you bolted from my apartment." Even slightly muffled through the door, his voice sounded as smooth as silk and sexier than sin.

"I'm busy, sorry," I called out nervously as I cautiously took a step toward the door, continuing to chew on my nail.

"Are you caught up with the birds again?" There was a hint of amusement in his voice as he fought to cough back a laugh. "From what I've read, it may be time to move on to the bees."

I brought my hands to my face and covered it, completely embarrassed. There was no way to pretend that this hadn't happened.

"So what do you say, can you open the door and we can talk?" he asked softly as if he knew what kind of fragile state I was in at the moment.

"I'm not opening the door so we can talk about… sex!" There was a panic in my voice as I felt the blush creep up my chest and quickly spread to my cheeks.

"Who said anything about sex?"

"You did," I stammered through the door, standing right beside it but still too afraid to open it. I wrapped my arms around myself to try to protect me from the judgment I assumed was radiating from the other side.

"I never said anything about sex. I said we should include the bees with your research on birds," he explained, and I could hear the amusement in his voice again. "You know, to be thorough."

I slowly opened the door and peeked around it to look at him. He was gorgeous. Just down right, drop dead, make-me-want-to-throw-my-panties-at-him-like-a-groupie-at-a-rock-concert-gorgeous. I sucked in a shaky breath and waited for him to talk.

"I thought you might need this back. You know, for all of your bird research," he said as he extended the notepad to me, forcing me to open the door further to grab it.

"Thank you." I nervously looked down at the notepad, avoiding his gaze as I took it from him and clutched it to my chest again.

"No problem, I wouldn't want you to lose all of your notes." He looked at me knowingly, holding my gaze as I tried desperately to look away. "Although I am curious to see how you use them."

He stepped forward, shoving his hands into his pockets as he watched my reaction. Without thinking, I licked my lips, his eyes immediately focusing on my them as his parted.

"Thank you, I appreciate you bringing this back," I said as I started to push the door closed. His foot popped in at the last minute, keeping it open.

"So, what were you really doing hanging outside of my apartment, taking notes?" He tilted his head slightly to the side and leaned against the doorframe. He looked so casual and easy-going which was the complete opposite of what I was feeling.

"It's stupid. Can't I just apologize for being such a creep and we can move on and pretend it never happened?" I allowed the feeling of defeat to take over my body as my shoulders slumped and a frown took over.

"We could, but I would much rather know why you're writing down all of the details of my sex life." He arched an eyebrow and waited.

I sighed heavily and closed my eyes. I didn't want to get into this with him. I didn't want to explain to him that I was so desperate for help with writing a few steamy sex scenes for my novel that I was willing to continuously eavesdrop on him having sex. I just wanted to hide my head in the sand and pretend that this had never happened.

"I'm still waiting," he said patiently. I opened my eyes and found him with his arms folded across his chest. A few seconds later, I heard the sound of high heels as they walked into the hallway, a subtle nod from him to the woman who had been in his apartment as she made her way to the elevator. He turned back toward me and smiled as he waited.

"Okay, fine," I sighed. "I'm an author and I'm struggling with a few of the sex scenes, so I was using your little sexcapades as inspiration for ideas of how to make it better." His eyebrows shot up high on his forehead as he pulled his head back in surprise.

"Sexcapades?"

"Yeah, you have quite a bit of extracurricular activities. And quite often, I might add. You might want to check to see if there's a world record that you're close to beating." I bit the inside of my cheek to keep from laughing as I watched the soft blush creep up his tan skin, feeling a little relieved that I wasn't the only one who was riding the embarrassment train anymore.

"So how many times have you listened to me have sex?" His question was direct and caught me completely off guard. Why hadn't I thought about the fact that I had just mentioned that this had happened more than once? I could have tried to blow this whole thing off as a one-time thing, but no, leave it to me to say too much and dig myself even deeper into the hole.

"It's kinda hard not to listen, you get pretty loud and the walls are pretty thin." I tilted my chin up and pulled back my shoulders, trying to regain any dignity that I might have left.

"You know, most people would just walk away to another room. Turn up the tv. Not write down, word for word, the details of their neighbor having sex." His eyes lit up as he talked and while it was still disturbing to me that we were still openly talking about his sex life, I felt relieved that at least he wasn't being a total dick about it. I wouldn't blame him if he was, he had every right to be.

"I didn't write anything down 'word for word'," I said, lifting my fingers in air quotes.

"May I?" he asked as he reached forward and grabbed the notepad from me, smiling as he took it and started reading. "So, *lift your ass so I can fuck you deeper*, wasn't word for word? What about, *oh God, yes, you're so fucking big. I love your huge cock!* Those aren't word for word?" He pulled his lower lip in between his teeth and studied me.

I felt my palms start to sweat again from his intense stare, afraid to look away and give him the upper hand of knowing he got to me.

"I was simply taking what I heard and turning it into something… better," I replied smugly, shrugging my shoulders as if I didn't care.

"Interesting…" He clicked his tongue against the roof of his mouth before looking at the notepad one last time and handing it over to me. "I'll try to be less distracting and keep my activities a little more discrete. Unless you are needing some more inspiration, then just bang on the wall a few times and I'll make sure I make her scream about how big my cock is."

I took the notepad from his hand as my jaw dropped, watching him walk back into the hallway as his cell phone started to ring.

"See ya later, bird lady," he said as he waved in my direction before turning his back to me and answering his cell phone. "This is Jax, what's the update?" His voice faded as he walked away. I stood staring into the empty hallway for a few seconds as I heard his door close and the lock click. What the hell had just happened?

Five

I spent the rest of the day obsessing over my interaction with Jax. First of all, how sexy was the name Jax? Second, why didn't I know what his name was before then? I was thankful to finally have a name to go with the sex god in apartment 2B, but I was surprised I hadn't heard any of the women calling it out during their love fests. Maybe he didn't bother to tell them and he really was paying women for sex.

I wrapped up the last few edits I had worked on and made sure I had saved my work once more before shutting down my computer. I had made a slight dent in the sex scenes that needed to be fixed but thankfully I had reached the halfway mark and still had a week and a half to work through the rest. It was almost 8 and my head felt likc it was going to explode from staring at the screen for so long.

I got up and pushed my chair under the desk and turned off the light next to the computer. No matter how much I might want to force myself to work more tonight, I needed to give myself a break and step away. It was late and I had once again, forgotten to eat at a reasonable hour. I wandered into the kitchen and opened the fridge, staring at the expired gallon of milk and a half-empty bottle of winc. Aside from that, the fridge was as empty as my head when it came to writing sex scenes.

I rolled my neck slowly, in an attempt to relieve some of the tension before grabbing the bottle of wine and calling it dinner. There was no need for a glass since I was planning to drown my embarrassment in Chardonnay. I headed for the couch and set the wine on the coffee table. I turned on the tv and scrolled through the limited options for something to watch. I picked up the bottle of wine and leaned back against the pillow as I got comfy, resting my feet on the coffee table. A flashback of sitting on the couch and pleasuring myself while I listened to Jax have sex crossed my mind, my body immediately remembering the way it felt when I imagined that it was me who he was talking to with that dirty mouth of his.

It was strange that I hadn't heard anyone come over since this was around the time that he always had his booty calls. Maybe it was because his schedule was different today and he hadn't gone into work? Or maybe I had creeped him out so much that he didn't plan to bring another woman back to his apartment ever again. I cringed when I thought about it, wondering how I would feel if I knew that someone was listening to me have sex. Would I be as easy-going about it as he was? There was a curiosity that had been evident on his face and I could almost guarantee that he would have stuck around longer to talk about it if I would have let him.

I shook my head to try to clear the thoughts from my head. This wasn't something that I needed to focus on. He had made it clear that whatever it was, was over when he walked away. And thank God he did because I don't know how I would have handled it if he had wanted to keep talking about it. I lifted the bottle of wine to my lips and took a sip, relaxing as the cold liquid made its way down my throat.

My stomach growled in protest, wanting something more than just wine.

There was a knock on the door which startled me for a second before I realized that it must be at his door. It was a little past the time that his booty calls usually showed up but apparently, it's never too late. I took another sip, trying to zone out and focus on the cooking show on tv when I heard another knock. This time, it was louder and definitely at my door. I pushed myself up off the couch and walked to the door, wine bottle still in hand.

As I opened the door, I was surprised to find Jax on the other side, holding bags of take-out food in one hand and a bottle of wine in the other. I raised an eyebrow in response, unsure of what he was doing there.

"I waited to see if you had ordered food tonight, but when it got past 7:30 and I didn't hear anyone dropping anything off, I thought I should find reinforcements." He lifted the bag up for me to see, forcing a delicious aroma to filter through the air and tease my appetite.

"You know my food delivery schedule?" I winced as I said it, realizing that I was not only boring and predictable but borderline pathetic. "I really have hit an all-time low," I whined as I stepped to the side so he could come inside. While I hadn't been expecting company, I couldn't complain about the surprise visitor especially when my stomach growled, loudly confirming how hungry I was.

"I'm not sure if me knowing when you get food delivered is worse than you knowing when I am having sex," he laughed as he came in and set the food and wine down on the kitchen counter. He turned to look at me over his shoulder, taking in the bottle of wine that was already in my hand. "Guess I'm a little late to the party," he teased, nodding at the bottle.

"No judgment, there wasn't much in my fridge to choose from other than this or expired milk and I was too tired to bother ordering food," I protested as I sat the wine down next to the bottle he brought.

"Well, then I guess I get to be your knight in shining armor. Or your Prince Charming? I don't know, whatever kind of hero you write about – I'm that guy." He winked and turned his attention to unpacking the food from the bag as I grabbed some paper plates from the pantry.

"I don't really write those kinds of books so you can be whatever kind of hero you want to." I smiled at him as I set the plates down next to him. "I do appreciate this though, thank you."

"You're welcome." He opened the containers and lined them up, side by side. "So, what kind of books do you write?" he asked as I got distracted by the food. The smell was heavenly as I eyed the contents of each container. There was a nice selection that he had brought but my sights were set on the orange chicken, my absolute favorite and total weakness when it came to Chinese food. He chuckled as he watched me lean forward, practically devouring the food before it was even on my plate.

I took the plate he handed me and stepped to the side to allow him to go first when I felt his hand reach behind and plant firmly on my lower back as he guided me to go in front of him to get my food.

"You can go first," I offered, trying to step out of the way.

"Absolutely not, ladies first." His hand was still firmly in place on my back, the warmth of it creating a different type of heat inside of me.

"You brought dinner, you should go first."

He pinned me with a look as his hand gently pushed me forward. I sighed dramatically as I tossed a smile over my shoulder before turning back to focus on the food in front of me. I scooped a small serving of everything onto my plate and stepped to the side so he could get his food. Suddenly it occurred to me that I didn't have an actual kitchen table which meant that we were either going to have to stand to eat, or we would have to sit next to each other on the small loveseat that I considered a couch. I rarely had company, so it never bothered me that I didn't have much furniture since it was always just me. The thought of sitting next to him in such close proximity sent goosebumps up my arm.

"Do you have wine glasses, or did you want to take turns drinking out of the bottle?" he asked, interrupting my thoughts.

"Oh, yeah. Sorry." I giggled nervously as I pointed to the kitchen cabinet next to the sink. He smiled warmly as he opened the cabinet and pulled out two glasses. "Do you want a glass, or did you want to keep drinking out of the bottle?"

"I'll take a glass, thank you." I felt the blush creep up my cheeks again as I imagined what he must have thought of me.

"No problem." He filled both glasses with the wine that was left in the bottle and set the bottle to the side. I saw the look on his face as he turned around to look for the table and realized that there wasn't one.

"We can sit on the couch if you want?"

"Sure, that's fine with me."

"Sorry, I don't have a lot of visitors, so I don't bother with having a lot of furniture," I explained as we walked over to the couch with our plates and glasses of wine.

"I don't have a lot of furniture either," He said as he set his plate on the coffee table and took a sip of wine before setting his glass down.

"Sometimes it just feels easier." I shoved a bite of chicken into my mouth to keep me from rambling on and sounding stupid.

"I agree. For me, it just didn't make sense since I knew I wouldn't be here long." He picked up his plate and leaned back against the couch as he took a bite.

"Are you moving somewhere else?" I asked, hopeful that it wasn't anytime soon.

"Na, but I'll be going back home soon."

The thought of him leaving soon made my stomach hurt. I was just barely starting to get to know him, I wasn't ready for him to turn around and leave right away.

"Where is home?" I asked in between bites, trying to avoid looking directly at him so I didn't choke on my food.

"Austin."

"As in, Texas?" My voice rose an octave as I struggled to hide my surprise at the news that he didn't live here.

"Yes ma'am. Born and raised."

"So, what are you doing here?" I asked as my curiosity got the better of me.

"I'm here on business."

"What do you do?" It felt like an interview with the constant questions as I desperately wanted to learn everything I could about this mysterious, sexy, stranger.

"I work for a housing developer. We build a lot of houses in Austin but the owner recently decided to test the market in Arizona so I was sent out here to start the process and see if it would be a viable project before they officially start."

"Sounds like an important job."

"It can be. If I make the wrong decision, it can cost the company a lot of money and wasted resources. If I make the right decision, it can make the company a lot of money. There's a lot of pressure that falls on my shoulders to make sure we make the right decision." He sighed before taking another bite.

"I can imagine how stressful that can be. So how are things going here? Will you be done with the project soon?" I tried to keep the desperation out of my voice that hoped he would be here for a little while longer so I could get to know him before he left.

"We actually received the proposal today and I delivered it to my boss before I grabbed dinner. Either he'll accept the deal he's offered, and we'll start building next month, or he'll reject it and I'll have to go back to the drawing board to see if there's anything I've missed. We can walk away from the deal, but it would be a huge blow to my career if we did."

"Why's that?" I asked as I set my empty plate down on the coffee table and brought my glass to my lips, taking a sip as he watched me.

"Because this was my lead. I was the one who pushed him to consider building out here. I had a tip from one of my buddies from college and this sounded like a no-brainer when I first proposed the idea to my boss. If we land the contract, then I'll get the promotion that I've been after. If we don't land the contract, then he can easily let me go."

"That easy—he'll just fire you?! That's crazy!" It blew my mind that his career seemed so fragile. I couldn't imagine having a career where I had to be that worried about whether or not I would still have a job if the deal didn't go through.

"Yeah, unfortunately. I've been there almost ten years. Started right out of college. But it's a culture of sales there and I'm not the only one that can do what I do. If I get the promotion, then I'll become a general manager that oversees this department and won't have to worry about my own leads anymore. That's what I've been working toward."

"That's intense. I'm sorry." I smiled sympathetically as I curled my legs up underneath me and took another drink of wine.

He leaned forward and set his empty plate on the table, exchanging it for his glass of wine as he leaned back against the couch and turned to look at me.

"No worries, but thank you." He took a drink and my eyes immediately focused on the way his mouth looked as his lips parted to allow the cold liquid to fill his mouth. Slowly, he lowered his glass and rested it on this thigh.

"So, back to my question before you got distracted by food, what kind of books do you write? Doesn't sound like you do the whole fairytale with the happily ever after thing."

"I write happily ever after, just not the damsel in distress types of books. I write about strong women who don't need a man to take care of them, and I pair them up with strong, broody, alpha males that challenge everything they ever thought they wanted." I smiled warmly as I thought about how I try to give each of my female characters the traits that I wish I had myself.

"How do I fit into these books?" he asked sheepishly as he lifted the glass to his lips to take a sip.

I froze in place, staring at him like a deer caught in the headlights.

"Oh come on, one of us had to mention it," he teased as he reached over and set his glass down.

"I was hoping we didn't have to," I laughed nervously, taking another drink. At this rate, I would be drunk and out of wine in no time. He eyed my glass and got up, walking into the kitchen and opening the new bottle before bringing it back with him. Without saying a word, he refilled both of our glasses and set the bottle on the table in between the empty plates.

"It's not that bad. I'm more… curious, than anything," he offered as he leaned back into the cushion. "Maybe a little flattered." He winked.

"It's not like I planned to do it. Honestly, it's not something that I would have ever done. Ever." I pulled in a deep breath as I tried to figure out how to explain myself without sounding like a complete sex depraved pervert. "I was struggling with trying to get new ideas and the next thing I knew, you were going at it with some girl on the other side of the wall and I realized that I could use some of it for my book. At first, it was just a one-time thing but then you kept bringing home a different girl each night and I found that I was able to get more stuff to use each time I listened in."

He smiled as he nodded his head, taking in every embarrassing detail that I had just laid out in front of him.

"I'm sorry, for what it's worth." I looked away to avoid the curious look that was crossing his face.

"Was it just the dirty talk? Or do you have some secret spy hole in the wall that you were using that I don't know about?" he joked, forcing me to choke on my wine. I turned to the side to avoid spewing it in his face.

"There is no peephole, I promise. Trust me, the dirty talk alone was more than enough to help me with what I needed."

His eyes went wide as I immediately regretted saying it. Why would I say that?!

"So, you're into dirty talk?" he asked, his voice low and sexy.

I blinked rapidly as I tried to think about how to answer that. Until recently, I would have said no but that was until I heard the filthy things I heard him say and realized how turned on I was from them. Either way, I wasn't about to confess to him that I was into it.

"It was just for my book," I lied, hoping he wouldn't see through it.

"Ah, I see." He nodded as if it made perfect sense to him even though his face confirmed that he didn't believe a damn word I said.

"What's that supposed to mean?" I turned my head to the side and glared at him, wondering what the smugness in his tone was supposed to mean. Did he just assume that I was into dirty talk or did he actually know what it did to me? Was I that transparent?

"Nothing. I just noticed the things you wrote down on your notepad were focused on the dirty talk, but you also had a few notes about sexual positions as well. I was just curious about how much of it was for the book and how much of it was for you." His look held me in place as he silently challenged me to respond.

"I just like to be thorough." I gulped.

"You know that there's nothing wrong with a woman being sexual and exploring her sexuality, right?"

I stared at him in disbelief. There was no way that I was sitting here, having this conversation with a stranger. He was bold and quite honestly, a little too cocky and sure of himself as he asked these intimate, private questions.

"Those are the kind of women that I write about," I replied as I took a drink and tried to avoid the question.

"Are you that kind of woman?" he asked, his voice low and sexy again.

"I don't see how that matters," I snapped, forcing my eyes to meet his.

"It matters because I think you are that kind of woman, but you don't allow yourself to be. I think you're very curious about a lot of things, but you shame yourself into thinking that it's not okay to explore them. To explore yourself. Find out what you like. What turns you on…"

I swallowed hard as I listened to each word, the ache between my thighs starting to build. I pressed my legs together and tried to focus on anything other than what this conversation was doing to me.

"You don't know what kind of woman I am. It was for a book. Simple as that."

"I think I do know what kind of woman you are. If it was just for a book, it wouldn't be so hard for you to write if you were allowing yourself to have what you want."

"And what's that?" I asked, watching as he licked his lips before speaking.

"Sexual freedom."

"That's not even a thing," I snorted.

"Wanna bet?" He arched an eyebrow and leaned closer to me. "I bet that if I leaned closer to you and whispered half of the dirty things you heard me say this afternoon, you would be wet and aching for me within seconds."

"That's awfully cocky of you and quite presumptuous that you think you know me that well when we barely just met."

"Honey, I have a way of reading women and you're an open book."

"I seriously doubt it." I looked away to keep him from seeing the truth on my face. I felt the cushion shift next to me as he scooted closer, the scent of his cologne in the air around me.

"So, if I were to touch you here, it wouldn't bother you?" He slowly ran a finger up my leg, stopping right below my knee. "Maybe if I went a little higher, closer to your throbbing pussy. Would that do it?" he asked as he leaned closer, his voice whispering next to my ear. I felt my heart beat faster as the ache between my legs started to increase. Why were these dirty words so arousing?

"You can tell me to stop but I don't think your body wants you to. Your mind is going to tell you to, but your body -- it's going to beg you to let me keep going. To get the release it craves every time you hear another woman coming hard on my dick." His hand slid higher, gently caressing my thigh. I tried to level my breathing, to focus on anything that would allow me to break free from this spell I was under and be rational.

"I would be willing to bet that your nipples are hard, pushing against the thin silk of your bra, desperately wishing it was my tongue instead."

I felt the rough prickle of the scruff of his five o'clock shadow as he leaned in and softly kissed behind my ear. Instinctively my body turned toward his, desperately wanting him to keep going.

"Your mind is desperate to hear the things I want to do to you while your body is begging for my hands to glide over it, caressing each spot before letting my tongue lick up every ounce of wetness as you ache for a release."

His hand slowly moved higher, skimming my stomach before moving up to my breast. My breath caught in my throat as I panicked on what we were about to do. Suddenly I felt his hand move away as he pulled back and stood up. He looked at me with sympathy as he chewed his bottom lip.

"Like I said – sexual freedom. It's amazing the impact it can have on you if you let it." He smiled softly as he turned and walked toward the door.

"How do you know that I don't want that? Or that I'm not already sexually free?" I asked as I questioned whether that was even a word or if I was so delusional that I was making shit up.

"We wouldn't be having this conversation if you were," he said with one hand on the doorknob. "But you know where to find me when you're ready."

I watched as he walked out and closed the door behind him. I sunk back against the couch, downing the rest of the wine in my glass as I tried to process what just happened.

<u>Six</u>

I had every intention of storming over to his apartment and showing him how sexually free I was but every time I got the nerve to do it, I would immediately talk myself out of it. Days had passed since I had seen him, likely because I was stalking him more now than I was before. The only difference was that now it was to avoid him at all costs. He still had a random girl come over every night around 8, but I no longer lingered by the wall waiting to see if I could hear what they were doing.

Friday night had come out of nowhere and my frustration was at an all-time high as I stared at the handful of unopened emails from my editor, reminding me that my updated manuscript was due back to her in a week. Needless to say, I hadn't made any progress since Jax left Wednesday night. My head had been clouded with thoughts about everything other than what I needed to focus on. I clicked the X at the top of the screen and closed out the document that I hadn't bothered to edit all day long and shoved my mouse off to the side.

I needed to eat but didn't feel like cooking nor did the idea of ordering delivery sound appealing so I grabbed my keys and cell phone off of the counter and made my way down to the little café across the street. I had been coming here since I moved in and sometimes would spend hours tucked away in a corner booth while I would write, tipping the wait staff generously for leaving me alone and only coming by to refill my coffee when needed. It wasn't a busy café to begin with, but it was even quieter on Friday nights which was just what I needed.

An older woman with short, curly gray hair greeted me when I walked in and nodded toward the booth in the back where I usually sat. I smiled and gave a quick wave as I made my way to the booth and plopped down. There were only a few other people in the café, scattered about so no one was right on top of each other. I loved that it always felt calm here, different than the busy coffee shops that I used to go to.

Moments later a waitress came by to take my order, which was easy given that I always ordered the same thing. I smiled as she walked away to go put it in and looked around when suddenly my eyes landed on a smile across the room that I would know anywhere. My heart started racing as I stared at Jax sitting across the room, laughing at something the blonde woman across from him had said. I looked beside me, trying to find a way to make myself invisible while I tried to figure out how to get out of here without him noticing me. The problem was that there was only one way out and I would have to walk directly toward him to get there. Obviously, he hadn't noticed me on the way in given that he only saw me from behind.

I took a deep breath and slowly slid over in the booth, pushing myself as close to the wall as I could get, hoping that he wouldn't look up and see me. There wasn't any reason for me to avoid him other than it would be awkward as hell to see him again after everything that had happened the last time I saw him. I let out a shaky breath, confident that I had camouflaged myself well enough that I could blend in with the booth when I saw his blue eyes land on mine.

His expression changed the second he saw me, forcing the woman to turn around and see what he was looking at. I pushed myself further against the wall and picked up my phone to pretend I was looking at something while I tried to block my face from their view. Coming out for a bite to eat was now officially the worst decision I had made all week. I kept my phone in front of my face and looked at my reflection, wondering what he saw in me compared to the woman sitting across from him.

She was gorgeous with long, straight blonde hair that swept across her shoulders, showcasing her toned shoulders. Her tan was natural with the tan marks to prove it as the strap of her black satin tank top slipped down her shoulder. I was the complete opposite of her. Her thin, very straight body was the complete opposite of my curvy body with big breasts and a big ass. My hair was so curly and unruly that I had given up on trying to straighten it years ago and embraced its natural texture which also meant that I didn't bother trying to color it. The natural red in it always found a way to show up regardless of what color I tried to go with so I learned to love the dark auburn color since I didn't have many other choices other than coloring it black.

I was still staring at my reflection, comparing myself to the woman he was talking to when I heard footsteps approach the table. Startled, I jumped in my seat and clutched my phone to my chest as I realized that it was just the waitress bringing my glass of water. I smiled and thanked her before setting my phone down and taking a sip. Cautiously, I leaned to the side a tad to peer around the corner, disappointed to find that Jax and the woman were no longer there. Probably for the best I thought as I took another drink of water, thankful that I didn't have to worry about an awkward interaction with him after all.

I sat quietly, tapping my fingers on the table as I waited for my food. A few minutes later I heard someone approaching and smiled as I looked up, expecting to see the waitress with my food. Jax smiled back as he slid into the booth across from me, folding his hands in front of him on the table.

"Mind if I join you?" he asked, showing no intention of leaving even if I said no.

"Do I have a choice?"

"Not really." He shrugged and looked over as the waitress walked over and slid the plate in front of me, looking confused as she noticed Jax sitting across from me.

"Can I get you anything else?" she asked as she looked back and forth between us.

"We're good, thanks," I said tightly, waiting for her to leave before turning my attention back to him.

"What are you doing?" I asked as I pulled off the paper wrapper and unfolded the napkin that was wrapped around the silverware. I picked up the fork and stabbed a piece of lettuce out of the salad, popping it into my mouth as I waited for him.

"Well, it seems we've been avoiding each other. Or rather, you've been avoiding me, so I wanted to fix that."

"I haven't been avoiding you," I lied as I took another bite, eying him suspiciously. Why did he care if we hadn't seen each other since the other night? He technically left the ball in my court. If he wanted something to happen, he could have stuck around and finished what he started.

"Really? Cause it seems like you have been."

"I've been busy."

"With the birds and the bees?" he teased as he leaned back and relaxed against the seat. His blonde hair was slightly mussed, and I wondered if it was from the blonde bimbo running her hands through it as they fucked before coming down here to ruin my dinner. I sighed heavily, gaining a look from him in response, as I acknowledged how ridiculous my jealousy made me and how I sounded borderline crazy.

"The birds flew south for the winter and the bees died." I pulled my lips into a thin line as I felt the stress roll over me once again as I thought about how far away I was from meeting my deadline.

"Wow. That sounds intense."

"It is." I could feel the energy-depleting from my body once again. I nodded toward the salad as a nonverbal invite for him to have some which was met with a nonverbal shake of his head. I shrugged and kept eating, thankful that I was putting something healthy in my body for once.

"Do you need help?" he offered quietly.

"Why? Do you want to go take another woman back to your apartment and have sex so I can listen in and be inspired?" I tilted my head to the side as I forked another piece of lettuce into my mouth. He laughed loudly, catching me off guard, and before I knew it, a smile was forcing its way onto my face as well. I rolled my eyes as I tried to ignore how ridiculous I had sounded.

"Not really what I was thinking, but if that's your thing then I won't judge."

"Okay, then what did you have in mind?" I asked as I finished my last bite and pushed the plate to the side before wiping my mouth with the napkin.

"I'm happy to come over and maybe we can brainstorm ideas. You can tell me what you have so far, and I can see if I can help make it hotter."

"That's not a word," I countered, sounding like a total ass.

"Sure it is." He winked. "Besides, I'm just putting the ideas out there, you're still responsible for making them sound good and polishing them up."

I pursed my lips together as I considered what he was offering. It wasn't such a terrible idea, was it? It wasn't like we were doing anything. Just talking about it and bouncing ideas off of each other.

The waitress made her way over to our table, sliding the check down as she collected the empty plate and silverware. As I reached for the check his hand darted out in front of mine, swooping it off the table before I could grab it. He held it to his chest and watched me, waiting for me to accept his offer before he would give me the check.

"Fine," I sighed. "You can come back to my place and help me. I'm sure you have better things to do on a Friday night, but be my guest."

I watched as his face lit up with a smile. I extended my hand for the check as he slid out of the booth and nodded his head for me to follow. As we got to the hostess station to pay, he slid the check down on the counter and pulled a couple of bills out of his wallet and tossed them on top of the check.

"Keep the change," he said to the hostess as he grabbed my hand and pulled me out of the café. There was a feeling of excitement running through me as we made our way back to my apartment.

<u>Seven</u>

"Okay, so read me the first scene that you need to work on," he said as he leaned back on the couch. It was odd and unsettling how he immediately made himself at home in my apartment, especially since it didn't bother me the way I thought it would.

I sat at my desk and pulled up the manuscript, scrolling through the pages until I found the first highlighted section. My shoulders started to get tense as I read the scene and what I had written. This was going to be embarrassing and suddenly I wasn't sure that I wanted to go through with it anymore. It wasn't just getting someone's help with something – it was letting someone into my private thoughts as they read the words that I had written before I was ready for the world to see them.

"It's pulled up over here if you want to come read it," I offered as I stood up and rolled my chair out from behind me. A sly smile formed on his beautiful face as he made no effort to get up.

"That's okay, I think this will work better if you read the scene to me."

"I think it's the same as you reading it yourself. Maybe even better that way so you can hear it in your voice."

"I don't think so," he said as he shook his head. "It will definitely work better if you read them out loud to me. I'll be able to process everything better that way and really get in the zone."

I pushed my lips together as I tried to figure out the logic behind his request, to find something that I was missing. I knew people had different learning styles but this just wasn't making much sense to me unless he really was more of an auditory learner and needed to hear it so he could process it instead of reading it.

"Is that your preferred learning style?" I asked as I continued to try to think through it in my head. I wasn't comfortable with him reading what I had written, let alone having to read it out loud to him. What if he had a learning disability that I wasn't aware of and wasn't being sensitive to? "Do you have trouble reading?"

My face turned beet red as I realized how rude I was with asking that. I'm sure the color of my face almost matched the color of my shirt leaving nothing to the imagination regarding how embarrassed I was. He laughed at my comment which helped to ease the tension that I had just inadvertently created.

"No, I don't have trouble reading. I read quite well, thank you."

"Then why are you so fixated on having me read it out loud?"

"Because if you read it out loud, it will be like you're talking dirty to me." His eyes lit up as he said it, a crooked smile pulled tight across his face.

"You're crazy. You know that, right?" I asked as I shook my

head and turned my attention back to the computer. "Do you want to come read this or not?"

I heard the sound of him getting up from the couch and walking over before I smelled the faint smell of his cologne as he stood right behind me. I was leaning forward to change the view of the page when I felt his hand on my lower back, sending chills through me at the sudden contact.

"Which part do you want me to read?" His voice was the low, sexy voice that threatened to make my knees go weak.

"It starts right here." I pointed to the screen; my body frozen in place under the warm heat from his hand. Slowly it moved down a little further as he stepped forward and leaned down to look at where I was pointing. His fingers twitched, reminding me that they were hovering right above my ass. My body fought the urge to move into his touch, to slowly adjust so his hand was on my ass instead of right above it. I wanted to have him bend me over the desk and plow into me as he read the words on the screen while bringing me to climax.

"You okay?" he asked softly as he turned his head to look at me. My body was tense, and I had to remind myself to let out the breath that I had been unknowingly holding from the moment I felt his hand on me.

"Yeah, I'm okay." My throat was suddenly dry, begging for something to coat it as my eyes drifted down his muscular body to the outline of a bulge in his pants. I let out a small gasp as I realized that he was hard right now and wondered if he was getting as turned on by everything as I was. He pulled his bottom lip in between his teeth as I looked up at him, afraid of getting caught staring but finding it hard to look away. I heard a faint chuckle before he turned his attention back to the computer screen.

"Alright, let's get started." He let out a sigh as he leaned in closer to the computer, his hand still firmly splayed across my lower back. "I quickly undid my bra, letting it drop to the floor as I stood naked in front of him. His bulging erection greeted me as he made his way over to me and carried me to the bed. We were tangled in the sheets within seconds, clawing our way to the release we both so desperately wanted."

I felt my temperature rising as my blood pressure skyrocketed from hearing him read it out loud. He slightly turned his head and arched an eyebrow at me before turning back to the computer.

"I could feel him coming undone inside of me, feeling relieved that I was able to give him what he needed." He stood upright and turned to look at me. "Is that it? That's the whole scene?"

"Yeah, I know. It sucks." I let my shoulders drop as I closed my eyes, hating that he officially knew how bad it was.

"It doesn't suck, it's just pretty quick and honestly, I think it's pretty shitty for her."

"Why do you say that?" I asked curiously. I had written this the same way that I had written all the others. There weren't that many other ways to write sex scenes other than adding in a few different details about the sex itself, but in the end, it always ended the same way.

"Because she is clearly horny and wants this dude to fuck her and take care of her." He gave me a pointed look that said that I should see where he was going with this, but I didn't.

"And?"

"And you didn't indicate that she got what she wanted. From how I read it – giving him what he wanted – means that she didn't have an orgasm and was okay with knowing she had given him one."

"So, what's wrong with that? That's real life. So is this book. It's not based on made-up stories of women who have orgasms during intercourse." I rolled my eyes much to his surprise.

"Wait—do you really think that women don't have orgasms during intercourse?" He turned to face me, arms crossed over his chest.

"I'm sure a few do, but the majority of women don't. That's just a fact." I folded my arms to match him and tilted my chin upward.

He blew out a frustrated breath as he studied me, processing something in his head that I wasn't sure I wanted to know about. Maybe this was a mistake to have him help me with this.

"I already know the answer, but I'm going to ask anyway. Have you ever had an orgasm during sex?"

I felt like my eyes were going to pop out of my head. What kind of question was that to ask someone that you didn't know that well? Hell, I wouldn't even ask someone I did know. People don't usually go around talking openly about their sexual experiences.

"I'm not going to answer that," I said smugly, turning to walk away when I felt his hand reach out and gently grab my arm.

"Hailey…" His voice was gentle as it trailed off into the air around me, sucking me back in and forcing me to turn around to look at him. "Has a man ever made you come during sex?"

I stayed silent, staring at him in disbelief. Part of me wanted to answer him, to talk about this because he made it seem like it was as normal and easy as talking about the weather.

"Hailey…" he coaxed, his eyes searching mine as I struggled with what I should do.

"There's not always time. You know how it goes, it only stays hard for so long so you kinda have to make the most out of the time you've got."

I watched his face fall as he let his hand fall away from my arm as he ran the other one across his face. He looked up at the ceiling as he subtly shook his head in disbelief.

"Don't look so surprised, it's not like it's a big secret that women fake it 99% of the time."

"Not with me they don't."

"You're awfully sure of yourself, aren't you?"

"Not at all. I'm very confident in my ability." He squared his shoulders and looked back at the computer screen. I didn't bother to respond because honestly, what do you even say to that? I had heard him through the wall several times, and honestly, the women didn't seem to have any complaints when they were with him. Either they were really good at faking it, or they were the lucky bitches in the 1% that didn't have to fake it.

"This is going to sound like a dick thing to say, but just hear me out, okay?"

I nodded and waited for him to continue.

"You can't write about what you don't know. And I mean that in a nice way. If you want to write the sex scenes that make people read them one-handed, then you have to learn about them yourself. Explore and find out what things turn you on. Find out what gets you off. Then take all of that information and put it into your books. People don't want real life, boring sex. They want to read about the stuff that they probably aren't getting at home. Or maybe they are? Who knows? Either way, you need to broaden your horizons or you're going to keep struggling with trying to write these."

I felt my shoulders rise and fall heavily with the sigh I let out, knowing that he wasn't telling me anything different than what my editor had been saying or what I had already been telling myself.

"So, what do you suggest? Should I rent some porn and invest in a vibrator or something?" I asked sarcastically knowing that there wasn't an actual answer to this problem. I was single and too busy trying to get this book done that I didn't have time to bother with dating, nor was I willing to do a one night stand with some random guy I met at a bar.

"While that does sound fun, I don't think that's going to help you much. A vibrator is nothing compared to having an actual dick inside of you. And while you may be good with using your own hands to pleasure yourself, it's not nearly as exhilarating as having someone else touch and tease you."

My jaw dropped open as I stood silent in front of him. There didn't seem to be anything that he was uncomfortable talking about and for a moment, I wished that I had that same confidence.

"I don't do that!" I shrieked as I walked past him and made my way to the couch, feeling the need to sit down before I passed out.

"Why not?" he asked as he came over and sat beside me.

"That's just not something that I do," I lied through gritted teeth as I looked away so he couldn't see the blush creeping up my face.

"Did you know that you blush every time you're caught in a lie?" There was a flirty, playfulness in his voice that I felt myself being pulled into.

"I'm not lying."

"So, you didn't bother to take care of yourself the other night when you were listening to me through the wall?"

"No. I just wrote down what I needed and moved on with my night." My voice was quiet, barely almost a whisper.

"That's funny because I heard another woman moaning through the wall. You know, they are very thin." He reached up and held the tip of my chin gently as he turned my face to look at him. "It was so fucking hot to think that another woman was touching herself, getting off to the sound of me fucking someone, that I came a second time."

His eyes were hooded as they turned a darker blue, the fullness of his lips amplified as he scraped his teeth over the bottom one. I glanced down and saw the bulge in his shorts, the outline of a dick that was hard and ready. A whimper escaped my throat as I felt the ache starting to build between my legs again. I wanted to reach down and rub until I got the release that I needed, desperate for someone to stop the throbbing. My breathing got heavier as I locked eyes with him, seeing the passion on his face as he waited for me to give him the okay. I sucked in a deep breath, hoping to pull in the courage I needed along with it as I quickly wrapped my hands around his neck and pulled him into me as my lips found his.

The kiss was anything but soft and gentle. It was urgent. Needy. Desperate. I wanted to do all of the dirty things I heard him talk about and I wanted to do them now. I parted my lips, allowing his tongue to plunge into my mouth, his urgency as intense as mine. My body turned slightly as I swung my leg over him and straddled him as we kissed. I pulled back for a second to catch my breath, allowing my head to fall back as he kissed his way down my neck and along my collar bone.

I rocked my hips and pushed myself down further, feeling the thick bulge beneath me as I desperately wanted to pull it out and ride it. He let out a moan as I arched my back and pressed down even deeper, his hands digging into my hips as I did. There was no doubt about it, we were going to have sex and it was going to be now. I was way too worked up to stop.

I leaned back and slid my hand beneath me to pull down his zipper when his hand reached around and grabbed my wrist, stopping me. I looked at him with shock and started to panic that he had changed his mind and didn't want to do this after all.

"We're not rushing through any of that," he growled as he pushed my hand down on his dick, allowing me to grasp it as he closed his eyes and hissed a quick breath out through clenched teeth.

"We're doing this the right way, you're going to come before we even start that." He quickly rolled me over off of his lap and onto my back before hovering over me and looking at me.

"You're so fucking gorgeous, you know that? I can't wait to have that curly hair wound around my fist as you scream my name for more." He grabbed the bottom of his shirt and pulled it up and over his head, tossing it to the side as his perfectly toned body stood before me. With one hand he undid the top button of his shorts and slid down the zipper, stepping out of them as he stood before me wearing nothing but boxer briefs that showcased just how big he is.

I licked my lips as I studied his body, every perfect little detail. He watched me like a hunter would their prey and slowly moved his hand down and grabbed his dick as my eyes followed every tiny movement. His eyes stayed focused on me as I watched his hand glide slowly back and forth over his shaft. The aching between my thighs was getting stronger the more I watched, finding myself more and more turned on by everything he did. His hand moved away as he reached up and hooked his thumbs in the top of his boxers, pulling them down as his erection sprung free.

As he kicked his boxers to the side, he moved his hand back to his dick and started stroking it again.

"Do you like watching me touch myself?" he asked as he licked his lips.

I nodded yes, too caught up in the moment to speak. My body was on fire and I felt like I might explode with the slightest touch.

"Take your shorts off," he instructed as he kept stroking, the rhythm hypnotizing. I froze as I thought about what he was asking but decided to push through it and do as he said. Quickly I unbuttoned my shorts and slid them down my legs before tossing them behind me onto the floor. I felt exposed as I laid on the couch wearing nothing but a tank top and a black lace thong. His eyes studied me as he roamed my body, taking in the view.

"Let your legs fall to the side and slide a finger inside of yourself."

My heart was racing as I followed his command. I closed my eyes as I let my legs fall open, slowly trailing a finger under the lace of the thong before sliding it inside and gasping at the sensation. Every nerve ending was on fire as I ached to be touched.

"Open your eyes and look at me," he said as he stepped closer. I opened my eyes and found him next to me, still sliding his hand up and down his dick as he watched me move my finger inside of me. "Fuck, Hailey, you're so fucking wet."

I nodded my head, wanting to say something back to him but my mind was completely blank as my finger slid in and out of my throbbing pussy.

"Take your top off," he growled, "your bra too."

I pulled my hand away and did as he asked, stripping myself to nothing but the thong. He let his hand fall away from his dick as he moved closer and stood above me. My round, full breasts were on full display as his eyes zeroed in on them. I watched as his eyes went wide as I ran my hands up my stomach and cupped each breast before flicking each nipple with my thumb. It was turning me on to see how turned on he was getting from watching me.

He slowly climbed on top of me as I spread my legs open to let him in. I could feel the weight of his body as he laid on top of me, bracing himself with his arm so he wasn't fully on top of me. He looked deep into my eyes, looking for any sign of reservation before closing his eyes and moving his head down to my breasts. I closed my eyes as I felt his tongue skim across my pebbled nipple before he pulled it into his mouth and began sucking. The sensation sent electric shocks throughout my body, bringing me closer to orgasm from sucking alone. I moaned as I arched my back and tried to shift my pelvis to line up so he could slide inside of me. I needed to feel him as he stretched me with his incredible size.

He sucked harder, creating pure torture as my body felt on edge. I reached down and grabbed his throbbing dick, desperate to have him fuck me. As I tried to line him up with my opening, I felt him push my hand away as he slipped a finger inside of me and pumped it hard and quick.

"Oh my god," I moaned breathlessly, right on the verge of coming on his hand. If his hand would shift slightly, I could use the friction of it to try to rub my clit and get the release I needed. His mouth quickly moved across and pulled the other nipple in, biting it before sucking it the way he had been sucking the other. I was in pure ecstasy and hell at the same time. He slid a second finger inside of me, making me gasp at the welcomed intrusion, as he pumped in sync with his sucking. I could feel myself right on the verge, desperate to let go.

"Please, please, please," I begged as I dug my nails into his back. "I'm so close, please…"

I could feel a rumble against my breast as he chuckled and sucked harder, removing his fingers and the pad of his thumb instantly found my clit and began rubbing it. Within seconds I felt the first ripple as my orgasm crashed through me, the intensity as I spasmed against his finger, riding every wave until it finally stopped, and my body sunk into the couch.

Holy. Fucking. Shit. He was not kidding when he said that he was confident in his abilities. I had only ever been with one guy and needless to say, orgasms weren't his specialty. Granted, I did get the mandatory birthday and anniversary special treatment where he would whine and complain about how long it took for me to come, but he never gave me one that was this intense. Hell, I hadn't ever given myself one either. I slowly opened my eyes and found him watching me with a smug smile on his face. "That was… I don't even know what that was. Amazing. Incredible… There aren't any words to describe it," I explained as I stared into his sapphire blue eyes.

"Liberating?" he teased as he smiled.

"I guess you could say that," I laughed. "Sorry you didn't get yours. We didn't have to do that, I was fine without one."

"Do you really think we are done?" He arched an eyebrow as he waited for me to respond. "Baby, we're just getting started."

I knew from experience that there was no way that he was still hard after having to wait that long, but I was willing to put in the work to try to get him aroused again so I could try to make him feel as good as he just made me feel.

"Well, I do know a few tricks to get this party started again," I said as I reached down to grab his dick. I gasped when I felt it rock hard, fully erect in my hand. I looked down as he slightly rolled off of me to show me that I wasn't just imagining it. "How is that possible?" I whispered more to myself than to him.

"Not all guys have the stamina of a 12-year-old boy who doesn't know what they're doing. Some of us can go quite a while." He licked his lips as he looked at me, desire etched on his face. "Some of us are willing to wait a few minutes to give the woman the best orgasm of her life before plowing deep into that wet pussy." He slowly slid a finger down my stomach and across my pussy before sliding it inside. I was still super sensitive from the indeed "best orgasm of my life", but the feeling of having him inside of me was something I needed now.

"How do you want it?" he asked quietly as he nibbled my ear while fingering me.

"You mean there's more than one way to do it?" I asked, laughing as he pulled his head back to see if I was serious. "I'm kidding!" I slapped at his chest and felt him laugh as he grabbed my wrist and pulled me on top of him as he sat on the couch. I was still wearing the thong as I straddled him, debating whether I should take it off before we got started.

"Leave it on," he said as if reading my thoughts. "It's fucking sexy to watch myself slid inside of you while you still have your panties on."

I nodded in agreement as I lifted and positioned myself on top of his dick. He hooked a finger into the side of my panties and pulled them to the side as I slid down, feeling the stretch as his dick filled every inch of me. I froze for a moment to adjust to his size, his fingers gripping my hips as he closed his eyes and adjusted to being inside of me. He was so big that it almost hurt to take all of him inside of me. I took a deep breath as I slowly rocked back then lifted slightly before sinking further down on his dick.

The feeling was incredible as I started to slowly rock back and forth, feeling him tight inside of me. He leaned forward and kissed my neck before moving back to my breasts, kissing and sucking each one as I continued to ride him. The pressure was building again, and I was desperate to grind against him in a way that put direct friction against my clit. Once I found the perfect spot, I rode him as fast and hard as I could, bringing myself to the edge as I felt him start to come inside of me. His body jerked beneath me as I tightened my muscles around him, feeling him dig his fingers into my thighs as he climaxed, taking me over the edge with him. My pussy spasmed around his dick, our bodies joined tightly in a sweaty embrace as we waited to come down from this new high.

I took a deep breath and opened my eyes, looking at the most gorgeous person I had ever met and for once – I didn't feel ashamed about what had just happened. Maybe I was riding an orgasm high, but I was proud of myself for giving in and letting something happen that I wanted to happen.

<u>Eight</u>

The weekend flew by before I knew it and Monday morning stared at me with an evil eye as the deadline was now only a few days away. Five days to be exact. I had made some progress on a few of the scenes, thanks to Jax, but every time we tried working through another scene, it led to us straight to the bedroom instead. My body was sore in the most wonderful way and my mind was distracted with the dirtiest thoughts that needed to go in my book if I could just get myself to write them.

It sounded simple- have sex and use the experiences to write what I needed to kick up the heat on the sex scenes in the book. The problem was that now that it was Jax and me who I was writing about, it felt way too personal to write about. It was different when he was just some random guy that I didn't know. Now he was Jax, the sex god and giver of multiple orgasms. Man of mystery and legend between the sheets. I couldn't possibly take anything from what we had shared and use it in my book.

I had struggled with it all weekend, but I didn't want to tell him that instead of him helping, in a way, he had actually made it worse. If he could have just stayed the secret neighbor that I spied on, I wouldn't have to worry about this being as personal as it was. I wouldn't have to be jealous that some other woman would read about my character's ridiculously huge dick and picture it thrusting inside of her from behind while he pulled her hair, while I knew that it was really Jax and not some made-up person.

I paced around the apartment while I waited for the coffee to finish brewing, remembering every place that we had sex in the last 48 hours. The couch. The kitchen counter. The rug by the balcony while the curtains were open. The shower. The bed. I looked back to the space that was supposed to be my safe place to work- the place where I could sit and the ideas would flow freely through my head before being typed out rapidly as my fingers raced across the keyboard. Now that safe place was clouded with memories of him bending me over the desk while he took me from behind as we watched ourselves in the reflection of the computer screen. Or the office chair that I rode him on while he ordered take out that he would eventually eat off my naked body while I laid across the coffee table.

I sighed as I picked up my cup of coffee and made my way to the desk. I was a professional. I could separate my personal life from a fictional life I was creating in my head. There wasn't any reason that I couldn't draw on parts of our experiences without having to include the entire thing. I opened the Word document and waited as the manuscript loaded. My fingers hovered over the keyboard as I waited for an idea to hit me. Anything.

I rolled my eyes and hung my head in my hands as I felt the wave of anxiety start to build as I thought about the deadline and how this was the first book that I might not finish on time. I stared off to the side as I looked at the bookshelf in the corner that had every book I had ever written and published.

Over the years I had dabbled in a few different genres and worked under a couple of pen names, but I never had this much trouble finishing a book. After Glen and I broke up earlier this year it felt like all of the love and romance just fell out of me and I haven't been able to find it again since then.

My phone vibrated against the wooden desk, shifting my attention from the screen. I looked down and swiped my phone open to find a text message from Jax, asking if I wanted to do dinner tonight. I quickly responded yes and moved my phone back to the side so I could try to focus. I spent the majority of the day on one scene and tried to think of how many different adjectives I could use to describe the same thing I had used before. It was pure desperation at this point, but thankfully this would still have to go through another round of editing before it would be published, and I was lucky enough to have a tough editor who would help me make this sound better than it was.

Before long it was already 6:00 and Jax confirmed he was on his way with dinner. I saved what I had been working on and instead of shutting down the computer, I turned off the screen and left it on. My goal was to try to relax some while Jax was there, then take another stab at trying to rework the few scenes that I still had left after he went home. The doorbell rang as I grabbed my phone and slid the chair under the desk.

"Hey, dinner smells good," I said as I opened the door and stepped to the side to let him in.

"And here I was thinking that you were going to compliment me first," he joked as he came in and set the bags down on the counter.

"Well, when you smell as good as that, I'll be sure to compliment you first." I winked and walked to the pantry to grab some paper plates and napkins.

"Now I see where your priorities are." He walked past and swatted me on the ass before leaning in and giving me a quick kiss on the back of my neck.

"I am starving…"

"Me too, only there's something else that I want to eat instead," he growled as he slipped his hand down the front of my shorts and teased me through my panties.

"Oh really? Well, maybe if you're a good boy, you can have that for dessert." I leaned back into him as his fingers lifted the side of my panties.

"Maybe I'll be a bad boy and have you as an appetizer." He slid a finger inside and held me in place as I gasped at the feel of his finger.

"You cheat, you know I'm too hungry to wait and too horny to say no," I whined as he pulled his finger out and popped it into his mouth, sucking it as I watched.

"Well then let's eat quickly so I can work on taking care of the good stuff."

"Sounds like a plan." I followed him the short distance to where he had set the takeout bag and bounced excitedly as I waited to see what he had brought that smelled so good.

"Tonight felt like a southern style BBQ kind of night, I hope that's okay?" He looked at me over his shoulder and returned the smile I was giving him.

Soon we were plopped down on the couch, watching tv as we stuffed our faces with ribs and all of the delicious sides he had picked to go with them. My stomach tightened as I stuffed it past capacity, instantly feeling anything but sexy. Thankfully he was just as full, so sex wasn't on his radar right now either. We stayed quiet while our food digested, cuddled up on the couch as he laid his head in my lap while I ran my fingers through his short hair.

"How did the edits go today? Did you get them wrapped up?" he asked when a commercial came on.

"I didn't make as much progress as I wanted, but I'm hoping to get them wrapped up soon." I shrugged to make it seem like it was no big deal. I didn't want to get into them with him and have to admit that I haven't been able to use any of the ideas he's suggested given that we had acted out each one. If I admitted to him that I couldn't write the scenes the way I needed to, without any attached emotion, then it would give away what the real problem was. I was getting too attached to someone who was like a ticking time bomb, never knowing when his time in Arizona would be up and he would be pulled back to Austin.

"We can work through them tonight if you want?"

"Thank you, I appreciate that. I'm gonna take a break tonight and give my head time to clear so I can focus."

"Okay, if you change your mind, just let me know." He shifted his attention back to the tv as the show we were watching came back on. I sat there, playing with his hair, as I debated whether I should tell him how I was feeling. I knew that this was just a fling or whatever you wanted to call it, but for some reason, it felt like more than that. It had only been a couple of nights since we had sex, but since then it felt like we were inseparable. When we weren't together, we were texting each other and checking in. He was at my apartment pretty much every opportunity he had when he wasn't at work. I didn't want to let my imagination run wild and turn this into something more than it was, but I also couldn't help but wonder what if it was something more than what I was giving it credit for. He hadn't had any of his booty calls over since we had hooked up and he was rarely on his phone when we were together.

My anxiety was starting to build so I quickly made an excuse to use the bathroom so I could clear my head for a minute. Being cuddled up with him on the couch after having dinner together felt like something that couples did. Not friends or next-door neighbors who were just hooking up. I was finishing up in the bathroom when I heard his voice in the other room, knowing that he had taken a call. They were expecting a decision on whether his manager was going to sign the contract for the Arizona deal any day now. I held my breath as I tried to listen before I realized that it was eavesdropping all over again and walked over to my bedroom window to give him some privacy.

After a few minutes, I was so lost in my thoughts that I hadn't realized that it was silent in the other room. I walked back into the living room, assuming he was done with his call when I saw him at the computer. His back was turned toward me as he focused on something. My stomach dropped when he moved slightly to the side and I saw the computer screen was on and the scene that I had been working on earlier was still open.

I tried to swallow past the lump that was forming in my throat as I walked toward him quietly, trying to figure out just how much of it he had read. His head whipped around when he heard my footsteps, an unrecognizable look on his face.

"What's this?" he asked as he pointed to the screen behind him.

I pulled my lips in as I closed my eyes. No matter how hard I tried, I would never be able to get that look on his face out of my head.

"It's nothing, I was just trying to clear my head earlier, so I wrote whatever came to me." I exhaled slowly, waiting for his reaction.

"She tried to wrap her head around the emotions that swam through her mind as she struggled to accept that she had fallen in love with someone who was unable to love her back. Someone who could promise her the world but couldn't deliver." He read the words on the screen out loud to me. "This is what came to you while you were trying to clear your head? I'm pretty sure this isn't the sex scene that we've been talking about or that your editor is expecting."

"It's not what it looks like." My eyes searched his trying to find the fun-loving Jax that had been replaced with the serious one who looked distraught in front of me.

"Is this how you feel? Is this about me?" He stared at me,

anger reflected in his eyes. "Am I really someone that is incapable of love and makes promises that I can't keep?"

"I don't know," I sighed as I threw my hands up in the air. "I don't know what to think or how to feel. I'm trying to figure it all out, but I can't. It's too hard, too complicated."

"Why is it complicated?"

"Because I don't know what this is. I don't have any idea how you feel. It's like you're this ticking time bomb and I don't know when you're going to explode on me when you up and leave, breaking my heart in the process."

His eyes softened as he listened, the truth falling heavily between us, shattering the façade that we had created.

"Breaking your heart." He closed his eyes as his shoulders fell. I looked away, ashamed to admit that I had fallen this hard for him so quickly.

"I know that it's stupid, I shouldn't feel this way and I'm trying to sort out what it means. Love is a complicated thi-"

"Love isn't an option for me. I should have been clear about that from the start." His tone was short as he shoved his hands into his pockets.

I felt like someone punched me in the gut as his words hit me.

"I'm sorry, I wasn't trying to put you in an awkward position. I just thought that maybe if you felt the same way, we could try to make this work until you have to go back," I whispered.

"I was on the phone with my boss when you went to the bathroom. He signed the contract so there's nothing left for me to do here. I'll be on a 6 am flight back to Austin tomorrow." He gave me a tight smile before shaking his head and walking out the door.

My world felt like it was crumbling beneath me as I stood alone in my apartment, trembling as the tears ran down my face while my heart shattered into a million pieces.

Nine

The next few days were blurred with heavy amounts of wine, chocolate, and coffee, in that order. My eyes were swollen, and I looked like shit. I hadn't slept Monday night after Jax walked out, which made it easier for me to hear the moment he left in the morning to catch his flight back to Austin. His apartment was eerily quiet, the sounds I had gotten so used to were now gone forever.

I tried desperately to work on what I needed to but I couldn't pull myself out of the depression I had allowed myself to sink into. After a handful of missed calls from my parents, my best friend, and my editor, I was officially worrying everyone. While it wasn't unusual for me to be quiet and keep to myself, it was out of the norm for me to avoid contact with every single person that I knew.

I shuffled around the apartment wearing a robe over my tank top and shorts I was still wearing since Monday when I heard the doorbell ring. I pulled the robe tighter around my body as I walked away, ignoring whoever was there. A few minutes later there was another ring followed by heavy pounding on the door which was guaranteed to get some complaints from my other neighbor.

I grumbled as I walked to the door and flung it open, surprised to see my editor at my door. She took in the sight of me with my unwashed hair piled in a messy knot on top of my head and raised her eyebrows. She leaned around me as she balanced her Coach handbag on her arm, taking in the dirty apartment behind me. As she stood upright, she looked me in the eyes and gave a sympathetic smile before walking in and setting her purse on the counter. I closed the door and turned to look at her, wondering what in the hell I had done to warrant this unexpected visit.

"What's up, Julie?" I asked as I walked into the kitchen and pulled another coffee cup out of the cabinet and set it on the counter next to the pot that was still brewing.

"I came to check on you, make sure you were still alive." She exhaled heavily as she looked around once more.

"You're my editor, you don't have to worry about me unless I miss the deadline." I placed my hand down on the counter and tapped my fingers as I impatiently waited for the coffee to finish.

"Yes, and I've been your editor long enough to know when something is wrong," she paused and looked around making sure that I saw her. "And something is wrong."

"It's nothing," I said as I waved my hand dismissively at her and started to pour the coffee.

"Hailey, talk to me." She looked up at me, her light brown eyes warm and inviting. "Let me help you with whatever is happening. As a friend, not as your editor." She placed her hand on top of mine and for a moment I felt like I might fall apart again.

I had been working with Julie for over five years and we had several successful books under our belts. We were right around the same age and even though it was a professional relationship, there were plenty of times where I felt like we could be friends. I never wanted to take advantage of our professional relationship, so I made sure to keep it that way. Purely professional.

"You don't have to do that," I said as my voice trembled.

"I know I don't have to. I want to." She smiled brightly as she grabbed one of the cups of coffee and followed me into the living room as we sat next to each other on the couch. She sipped her coffee while giving me her full attention as I told her all of the painful details of Jax and everything that had happened. She giggled when I told her about the part where I was eavesdropping on him having sex and using it in my books. A quick I knew it! was all she said before she leaned back into the pillow and listened as I told her the rest. As I got to the end, I watched as her smile faded and her eyes filled with sympathy for me.

"So that's it. I was stupid and I let myself fall for a guy who had no intention of doing the same." I shrugged my shoulders and looked away as I took a long sip of coffee, trying to soothe the ache that was threatening to destroy my heart again.

"I'm sorry, Hailey, that's a lot to have happen in such a short time."

"Thanks. It's my own fault though. I never should have allowed anything to develop between us. I'm not the kind of girl who can do no strings attached, casual sex. I never have been." I pulled my bottom lip in between my teeth, biting down hard to try to force away the tears that threatened to come back as memories of another time in my life sprung to mind.

"I get it, I really do." She nodded and smiled softly.

"Well, that's it. That's where I'm at and why I can't rewrite the scenes that we need and why I'm going to miss the deadline and throw my career out the window," I said in one breath, pulling another one in right after. I leaned over and set the empty coffee cup on the table with a shaky hand before folding my hands in my lap and making eye contact with Julie.

"You're not throwing your career out the window, nor are you missing your deadline," Julie said as she rolled her eyes and stood up. She held a hand out for me, waiting for me to take it. "Well, come on, let's go!" There was a new enthusiasm to her voice that I hated. I grunted as I took her hand and let her pull me up.

"Okay, I'm up. Now what?" I asked with a little too much sarcasm in my voice.

"Now you sit your ass down at your desk and we work on those edits. TOGETHER." She smiled as she pulled the chair out and waited for me to sit. I looked around for something for her to sit on before remembering that I didn't have much in the way of furniture. "I don't have an extra chair, do you wanna sit here?"

"Nope, I'm good standing. It's good for my posture," she assured me as she leaned forward, letting her short brown hair fall forward before tucking it behind her ear. She was a very attractive woman, tall and slender, with delicate features but killer heels. I had no idea how tall she really was but every time I saw her she was in 5-6 inch heels and still not much taller than I was.

I leaned forward and turned the computer on, waiting for everything to load while we waited. I glanced at her out of the corner of my eye, admiring how put together and polished she looked, while I looked like I should be taken outside and hosed off before being allowed on the couch.

A few seconds later the screen finished loading and the manuscript popped up before us. I was embarrassed that I hadn't been able to work through the things I had told her I would. Maybe now that she knew everything that had happened she would take it easy on me and not hold me to the same high standard that she always did.

I scrolled through the pages until I found the first highlighted section and stopped. I didn't have to read it to know that it was the paragraph that Jax had read before he stormed out and never came back. I swallowed hard and ran my palms down my shorts as my hands started sweating. I looked at Julie out of the corner of my eye and saw her eyes narrowed in on the words on the screen in front of her. Once she got to the end, I saw her face fall when she knew why I couldn't write what I needed to. Before there was no emotion, it was just made up sex between fictional characters. Now it was emotional sex between real-life people.

A few hours later we had worked through the rest of the scenes and made the last few corrections that she had suggested. It felt amazing to be done and to no longer have this hanging over my head while I was trying to process everything else. For the first time in weeks, I felt like myself again and there was a small bit of hope that maybe I would snap out of this funk that I was in. I barely knew Jax a week before I fell for him, I shouldn't be this worked up over it. My biggest flaw was that when I fall, I always fall hard.

I got up and let Julie take over the computer so she could email herself the file and check an email she was waiting for. It was close to seven and I realized that we had worked throughout the day without any breaks. I had been so depressed lately that eating was the last thing I had been thinking about, so I hadn't paid attention that we had spent the entire day working without lunch.

"Alright. We are all set," she said as she got up and pushed the chair back under the desk.

"Great. Thanks again for your help. It's a huge relief to have that one done." I smiled back at her.

"No problem, I'm glad I could help."

"I'm sorry that I sucked up your whole day, can I buy you dinner as a thank you?"

Her shoulders slumped as her face fell, a look of sadness suddenly appearing.

"I'm sorry, Hailey, but I can't. Thank you for the offer though, that's very generous of you."

"Is it because I look homeless? I can go clean up really quick, it won't take long," I said as I pointed over my shoulder toward the bathroom.

"No, not at all. You're beautiful, don't ever think otherwise," she smiled as she sucked in a deep breath and slowly let it out before continuing. "I can't do dinner because I have to get on a 9:45 flight to D.C. I have a second interview with a large publishing house, and if it goes well, I'll be moving there next week to start a new job." She smiled nervously as she waited for me to process the news.

"You're leaving?" I subtly flicked my fingers a few times as my hands hung by my side to keep them from trembling.

"If I get this job, yes. It's a really big opportunity for me." Her voice was quiet as she spoke.

"Well, I wish you the best of luck. I'm sure you'll get it, you're the best," I choked out, trying to hide the crack in my voice.

"Hailey, I'm so sorry. I didn't mean to spring this on you like this. I wanted to tell you in person, that's one of the reasons that I came by," she walked toward me and held her hands out for me to take. I gently placed mine in them and felt the warmth as she squeezed them and smiled. "I wasn't about to leave without making sure that you got those edits done, and I felt terrible that it was my fault that I had to bump up your deadline."

I looked at her puzzled. What did she mean that she had to bump up my deadline? I knew I had been walking around in a fog but I was pretty sure it was still Wednesday and that I still had until Friday night to get the edits to her.

"What are you talking about?"

"Didn't you get the email that I sent Monday night? It explained that I would be traveling today and would need the completed manuscript by tonight at 7:30."

I thought back to Monday night and knew why I hadn't seen it. After Jax had read what I wrote I had turned off the computer screen and didn't bother to turn it on again until this morning. My usual routine was to check my email first thing every morning but I hadn't been doing any sort of a routine the past few days.

"I didn't see it, I'm sorry, I haven't checked my email since Monday morning," I said quietly, feeling ashamed that my personal life had completely fallen apart to where I wasn't even able to function the way I usually did.

"It's okay. We still got it done and I was able to submit it to my team before the deadline. It was close, but we made it." She laughed and I was thankful that she had shown up unexpectedly and helped me through the edits.

"When will I know whether you'll be back or not?" I asked nervously, not wanting to know the answer. Julie was the only editor that I had worked with since I started my writing career and the idea of working with someone who didn't know me frightened me.

"I'll touch base with you this weekend and give you an update. They're supposed to decide by Friday."

I nodded as I struggled with what to say next. I hated goodbyes; I was terrible at them. They were awkward and uncomfortable regardless of who they were with and how you felt about it.

"Well, I better get going." She said as she checked her watch before walking over to get her purse. "We'll talk soon, okay? Be sure to take care of yourself in the meantime." She pulled me into a quick hug then she was out the door and I was left alone in my quiet apartment.

The longer I stood there staring at the door, the more I realized that I needed to do something to get myself out of this mood. I jumped in the shower and cleaned up, feeling ready to take on the world. Thirty minutes later I gave myself a quick once over in the mirror, making sure my curls were perfectly lined up to frame my face while smoothing down my denim skirt and lacy black tank top. I smiled and reassured myself that I deserved a fun night out as I grabbed my cell phone and keys and made my way to the elevator.

A few minutes later I was walking out into the hot evening air with my head down as I texted my best friend to see where she wanted to meet up for a drink. I stepped to the side to get out of the way while I finished typing when I felt a hand softly touch my lower back. I stilled, knowing who it was without having to turn around. His scent invaded the air around me, making it hard to breathe.

My body stiffened against his touch, immediately ready to run and get away from the heartache that was lurking behind me. I slowly blew out the breath I had been holding as I tucked my cell phone into my front pocket and debated on whether to turn and face him.

"Hailey, can we talk?" His voice was low in my ear, sending chills down my arms. It took everything I had in me not to turn around because I had no idea what would happen if I did. There was a good chance that I would wrap my arms around him and kiss him but there was a better chance that I would punch him. I pulled my shoulders back and held my head high as I walked away, hearing him calling my name in the distance.

<u>Ten</u>

My heart was still racing as I focused on the sound of my five-inch heels clinking against the concrete as I made my way into the bar and scanned the room looking for Amanda. She was hard to miss with platinum blonde hair that she kept in cute pixie style which suited her features perfectly. Off in the corner, I saw a hand lift and wave, her beautiful smiling face watching me as I made my way over to her.

"Wow! Girl, you look like you're trying to make someone eat their heart out tonight!" she squealed as I leaned in for a quick hug before climbing up on the barstool across from her.

"Thanks, I felt like getting a little dolled up tonight," I smiled and pulled the drink menu out of the holder in the center of the table. I scanned the menu knowing that I already knew what I wanted. It was the same thing that I always got.

"I hope you don't mind but I took the liberty of ordering you a drink." She squinted her face up as if she expected me to get mad.

"I don't mind at all, it's not like I was going to order anything different," I laughed and set the menu down on the table at the same moment the waiter came over and set our drinks down in front of us. I smiled as I waited for him to move before reaching forward and grabbing one, the smell of lemon already intoxicating.

"Cheers," Amanda said as she lifted her glass to mine, clanking them in the air before we both took a sip and sighed.

"They have the best lemon drops," I sighed as I set the glass down in front of me.

"Yeah, they really do. I'm glad you asked to meet up tonight, I thought for sure you'd be holed up in your writing cave for a few more days until your deadline."

"Turns out my deadline had been moved up to tonight and I didn't know it until after Julie stopped by and helped me crank everything out. It's officially wrapped up and as much as I love Drake and Allison's story, I don't want to see or hear about them again anytime soon," I snorted and lifted my glass for another drink. Amanda laughed along with me as she started talking about a random love triangle that she had heard about at work. Her hands flew around in the air wildly as she animatedly told the story about how someone got caught in the act and instead of the woman getting mad, she just joined them. Normally, I would have listened more attentively and made mental note of what I might be able to use later on in a book.

As I tried to keep up with what she was saying I couldn't help but be distracted with thoughts of Jax. Why did he come back? Was he even there or had I imagined him in a bout of desperation? Did I miss him so much that I was hallucinating that he was actually there? There were so many thoughts racing through my head that I couldn't focus on what she was saying and totally missed what was going on when she turned to glare at me, busting me on the spot.

"Are you even listening?" She asked, irritated.

"Of course I am, you know better than that," I lied, hoping she would believe me and keep going. She kept watching me as she started to talk, making sure I was paying attention. I tried to focus the best I could, but my pocket started vibrating against my thigh which immediately pulled my attention away. I forced myself to ignore it, to not give in, and pull my phone out to see if it was Jax. The longer it vibrated, the harder it was to focus.

"Oh for fucks sake, just answer your phone already," she blew out as she nodded toward my pocket.

I rolled my eyes and leaned back, fishing my phone out as she waited for me to check it. There were seven missed calls and eight unread text messages, all from Jax. My heart skipped a beat as I wondered what he was calling for. It seemed he was feeling pretty desperate to talk to me which instantly sparked my curiosity.

"Everything okay?" she asked, forcing my attention back to her and away from my phone.

"Yeah, it's nothing." I shook my head and laid my cell phone face down on the table in front of me. She watched me warily while she waited to see whether she should start talking again. I gave her a look, encouraging her to go on, and tried my best to focus and listen. Not even a full minute later, my phone started vibrating across the table, immediately grabbing her attention again.

I swallowed hard, knowing how this was her biggest pet peeve and hating that I wasn't able to do anything to stop it. Even with my best efforts, I still couldn't pull my attention away from Jax. I watched with terror as she reached forward, grabbed my cell phone, and slid the button to answer it. My jaw dropped in disbelief as I stared at her.

"This is Hailey's phone, is this the asshole who has her all twitterpated while I'm trying to spend some quality time with her?" she asked into the phone while slapping my hands away as I tried to grab it from her.

I sunk into the barstool and covered my face in my hands knowing that the damage was already done. It didn't matter now that Amanda had Jax on the phone, there would be no intervening and no saving myself from the conversation we were guaranteed to have as soon as she was done.

I didn't bother trying to hear what was being said on the other line as Amanda turned her head and looked at me, shocked by whatever she was being told. I picked up my glass and downed the rest of my drink, feeling comforted as the liquid made its way down, leaving a trail of heat in its path as the alcohol started to take its effect. I flagged the waiter down as he passed by, pointing to the empty glass to request another one. A quick nod and then he was off to put in the order. I was going to need the liquid courage to keep going with where this night was headed.

"Well you sound like a real asshole," Amanda sneered into the phone as she rolled her eyes and hung up. She slid my phone back across the table to me and shifted her eyes to the waiter that was on his way to our table with another round of drinks. As soon as the drinks were on the table, I snatched one up and started drinking, hoping I would soon be too buzzed to have to deal with anything for the rest of the night.

Amanda watched me out of the corner of her eye as she slowly took a sip of her drink. I could already see the wheels turning as she tried to piece together everything with Jax and more importantly- why I hadn't told her about him. It wasn't unusual for me to go a few weeks without talking to her, especially when I was up against a deadline. But Jax, that was something that I wouldn't usually keep from her and she knew it.

I finished the rest of my drink and set the empty glass on the table, subtly shaking my head no at the waiter as he walked by. I definitely didn't need any more refills tonight. I tapped my fingers nervously against the glass as I tried to avoid looking directly at her. Once I made eye contact with her I would cave and tell her everything that I had been working so hard to bottle up.

"You know we're not leaving here until we talk about this, right?" Her tone was firm but not aggressive, which I was thankful for. She sounded more like a concerned friend and less like the lecturing mother I was expecting.

"I know," I sighed.

"So, who is Jax and why is he trying to find you so he can explain what happened?"

"He's my next-door neighbor." I looked past her to the front door as it opened, and a couple of rowdy frat guys made their way in and plopped down at one of the empty tables behind us. "WAS my next-door neighbor. He doesn't even live here, he lives in Austin."

I shifted uncomfortably in my seat, remembering how much I had hated hearing him talk about going back to Austin, but how I kept hoping that I would have more time with him than I did.

"Okay, so what's going on with the neighbor? He sounded really upset, Hailey." Her eyes soften in the dim lights above us, casting a warm glow on her face.

"It's a long, complicated story," I sighed, not wanting to get into all of the details.

"So then give me the short version. Headline news it for me."

"Fine. I had writer's block and couldn't write a few love scenes to save my life. He's a man whore and had a different girl over every single night. I started listening in, got inspiration for the book, and didn't know when to stop. He caught me. It was awkward at first but then he was more curious and intrigued about the process. Things happened and for a very brief moment, it felt like we were a couple," I said in one breath as my lip trembled. I sucked in a deep breath before I forced myself to continue. "Except that I was the only one who was feeling that way. He made it clear when he found out how I felt about him. About us."

"Did you try to talk to him about it after you told him?"

"I didn't tell him. He read about it when he saw it on the computer. I had written about it in my manuscript, just messing around. I couldn't get the sex scenes out so I wrote what I could and that's how he found out. He said he wasn't capable of love, or some shit like that, and walked out and left." I pulled my lips together in a tight smile and looked at her.

"Oh, Hailey..." She reached over and gently squeezed my hand.

"I'm so sorry, I know that must have brought up bad memories when he walked out."

"It did," I admitted.

"Did you tell him about what happened with Glen?" she asked cautiously.

"No. It wasn't something that he needed to know."

"Really? You don't think that he needs to know what happened with you and Glen?"

"No," I snapped, "I don't think anyone needs to know that the only man I've ever loved— my high school sweetheart who I lost my virginity to— left me at the altar on our wedding day because he didn't know if he could spend the rest of his life with me. He didn't just break my heart— he shattered it into a million pieces that I will never be able to put back together again." I felt a sob escape my throat as I held a shaky hand in front of my mouth, trying to keep it together. It had been six months since it had happened, but it still hurt as bad as it did that day. Only for a brief moment, it had felt like Jax was capable of helping me put my life back together again.

It had only been a few months since Glen walked out on me and I hadn't been able to write a love scene after I caught him with another woman a few days after he broke things off with me. Seeing him making love to her was devastating and every time I tried to write about sex, all I could see was them. Naked. On our bed. They laughed as I cried and ran out of the apartment, never bothering to look back. I left the majority of my stuff there and didn't bother to buy new stuff when I moved into my apartment. Why bother? The only friends I had, aside from Amanda, were friends we shared who stopped talking to me after we broke up.

"Having Glen leave you was a terrible thing to go through, but Hailey I was there for all of it. He did you a favor. You're a better person because of it. You're a stronger woman. And honey, you deserve love and you're more than worthy of it."

Her last sentence broke me. I felt the air get sucked from my body as I crumbled at the table, not giving a damn that everyone was looking at me and watching. I'd spent so much of my life worrying about being what everyone else wanted me to be that I never stopped to be who I wanted to be. I felt Amanda's arms wrap tightly around my shoulders as I cried.

A few minutes later I forced the air back into my lungs as I tried to calm myself down. So much for getting dolled up for a night out if I was just going to ruin it by having a breakdown in the middle of the bar. I was thankful that Amanda was willing to change the subject to something else for the remainder of the night, not forcing me to talk anymore about Jax or Glen.

I felt a yawn take hold of me, reminding me of how little I had slept in the past few days. We said our goodbyes and I promised to call her tomorrow as I jumped in the cab and made my way back to my apartment. It was a short enough walk that I could have walked back but my feet were killing me and I was exhausted.

The cab stopped in front of the entrance to my building, waiting long enough for me to tip them before speeding off. I stepped into the elevator and leaned my head back against the cold wall as I saw my reflection in the mirror. Given the massive breakdown I had earlier I didn't look too bad, even in the worn-out mirror in the elevator. The elevator dinged as it came to a stop, the doors slowly opening after that. I stepped out into the hallway and dug my keys out of my front pocket

As I turned the corner I gasped when I looked down and saw Jax leaning his back against my door, legs stretched out in front of him. I had no idea how long he had been sitting there waiting for me, but it had to have been a while if he was already asleep. There was no way for me to open the door and go inside without waking him up.

I cleared my throat loud enough to wake him, watching as he stirred and looked around confused. Once he saw me, he pushed himself up off of the floor and stood in front of me. His eyes quickly scanned my face and I saw worry lines etch into his when he saw that I had been crying. Self-consciously I looked away.

"Hailey, can we please talk?" He pushed his hands together in front of him as he begged.

"There's nothing to talk about. It's late and I'm tired," I said as I stepped past him and shoved the key in the lock, jiggling it a few times to get it to go in all the way. Finally, the lock clicked, and the door swung open. I wasn't in the mood to deal with everything with him right now, but I also didn't want him to leave. It felt nice having him there, even if I was still hurt and pissed at him.

"Why don't you just go back to your place and we can talk tomorrow?" I rubbed a hand down my face suddenly feeling more tired than I was a few minutes ago. Being around him felt calm and easy which made it hard to want to stay awake right now. Cuddling up against his warm body sounded delightful but it wasn't an option, so I quickly forced the thought out of my mind before I did something stupid.

"I don't have a place anymore. They went ahead and canceled my lease early and my stuff has already been shipped back to Austin." He rocked back on his heels nervously as he said it. "I have a hotel room, and I'm happy to leave if that's what you really want."

I stayed quiet and looked past him, shaking my head as I tried to figure out what it was that I wanted. I was too tired to deal with these emotionally driven mind games that he was playing. First, he freaked out that I was starting to have feelings for him and left, then he showed up to my apartment at two in the morning, asking to talk. I wasn't in the mood for this emotional roller coaster.

"I'm too tired to ask why you're here and not in Austin. You can sleep on the couch, but you need to keep your clothes on. And I mean ALL. OF. THEM. I don't need to come out here and find you sleeping in your underwear." I pointed a finger at him and shook my head.

He smiled and nodded, trying to hold back a laugh that was threatening to come out. I sighed as I tossed a blanket at him and went to my bedroom alone. So much for getting some rest tonight knowing that Mr. Sex God was going to be sleeping on my couch and was only a few feet away.

Eleven

I woke up to the smell of coffee brewing and bacon frying on the stove. I turned to look at the clock on my nightstand, feeling way too tired to get up and try to function today. It was already after nine which meant that I needed to get up, even if I didn't want to. Granted I didn't have to worry about making the deadline anymore, I still needed to start working on some of the marketing tasks for the new release.

I climbed out of bed and gave myself a quick glance in the mirror before walking out into the kitchen. Jax was standing at the stove wearing the same outfit he had on last night, cooking. I took a moment to admire the view in front of me as he leaned forward, his T-shirt stretched tightly across his back and shoulders. He had a killer body, but the shorts he was wearing showed that he also had a great ass. Why hadn't I noticed that before?

I walked quietly into the room, debating on whether I should go put a robe on or at least put some real clothes on. I was wearing a thin worn out tank top with a pair of short cotton pajama shorts. It was my favorite outfit to sleep in because it was light and comfy, but now that I thought about it, it didn't leave much to the imagination. Not that he had to guess what I looked like, I just didn't want to come across as desperate or like I was begging for it.

"Good morning," he said as he glanced at me over his shoulder and smiled. "How did you sleep?"

"Pretty good, I was exhausted. Did you sleep okay on the couch?"

I felt bad for making him sleep on the couch when my bed was plenty big enough for both of us. The problem was that I didn't trust myself around him. One look from him would be all that it would take for me to let my guard down and trust him. And that was a risk that I couldn't afford to take right now.

"I slept as good as I could, given the situation." He kept his back to me but I could see the tension in his body as he said it.

"I'm sorry, it's not the most comfortable to sleep-"

"It wasn't the couch, Hailey, it was you." He turned around and looked at me, a stoic expression on his face. I clamped my jaw shut and stared at him, waiting for him to explain what that was supposed to mean.

"I couldn't sleep knowing that you were in the other room and I couldn't touch you. I couldn't hold you as I heard you cry. I couldn't comfort you knowing that I was the one who caused you pain. It killed me that I'm the reason for all of this, so no, I didn't sleep very well last night." His face was somber as he turned back to the stove.

For once I didn't have the words that usually came so quick to me. I was completely stunned by his admission and confused by everything that had happened in just a few days. What had changed his mind about how he felt after he stormed out Monday night?

A few minutes later carried two plates of food over to the coffee table as I followed behind him with the cups of coffee. We sat down and I turned to look at him, ready to confess everything that I needed to get off of my chest when he put his hand up to stop me.

"Eat first, talk after." He closed his eyes and took a deep breath as if the sight of me was hard for him to look at.

Self-consciously I leaned back against the couch and hid behind a pillow that I used as a lap tray for my plate as we ate in silence. The food was delicious but simple. Bacon, eggs, toast, and some hash browns had me full in no time. After I finished, I set the plate on the table and grabbed my cup of coffee, retreating to my hiding spot behind the pillow. It seemed that he had something on his mind that he wanted to talk about so I was going to stay quiet until he did.

He got up and cleared our plates, taking them to the sink before coming back and wiping his hands down the front of his shorts. He was completely nervous, which would usually be adorable, but given that this involved me as well, I found it to be nerve-wracking as I waited for him to get on with it.

He sat down on the edge of the couch and turned to look at me. The way the sun filtered in through the sheer curtains made his eyes sparkle like the ocean.

"Hailey, I am so sorry about what happened the other night," he breathed out. "I was stressed with work and I got a little freaked out by what I read. But still, I should have stayed and talked to you instead of just leaving."

I watched him quietly, not giving anything away about how I felt. Honestly, I didn't even know how I felt about it anymore. The lines between what happened with Jax and what happened with Glen had blurred so much in the past few days that it was one big, sloppy mess.

"I didn't want to fall for you. I purposely tried to avoid you for that exact reason. I was watching you long before you even noticed me. I knew when you were in a good mood when I would hear you crank your music up and sing along at the top of your lungs. I knew when you were having a bad day based on when you ordered your takeout. If it was early in the day- it was a bad day. If it was late in the day, it was a good day and you were too busy to stop and eat." He smiled at a private thought and then continued.

"You are gorgeous, and you walk around as if you don't care whether anyone notices you or not. That's so fucking sexy and different than the girls I usually meet who are so stuck on themselves that they feed on knowing when someone is watching them. You're carefree and quirky. Playful and sexy. And dear God, if I would have known that you went to bed by yourself last night wearing that- you would have had to use a stick to beat me to keep me out of your bed." His eyes trailed down my body sending shivers up my spine from the intense look.

"I've never been the kind of guy who thought he wanted a commitment. My mom cheated on my dad and ran off with another man when I was four. I watched him struggle as a single dad as I grew up, watching everything he sacrificed to give me a better life. He passed a few years ago but before he did, I made him a promise that I would go after every dream I ever had, and I would do something big with the life he gave me. I owed it to him." He took a deep breath and I could tell that it was hard for him to talk about his father, the pain he felt from losing him still raw and fresh. "I don't do relationships because I haven't lived up to the expectations that I set for myself and I can't afford any distractions. I can't break the only promise that I ever made to my father." His shoulders dropped and for a minute I worried that this was it, this was what he came to tell me. He couldn't be with me because I would be too much of a distraction and he would let his father down.

I sucked in a ragged breath and held it as he stood up, bracing myself for him to walk out and leave me again. Instead, he paced back and forth in the small space between the coffee table and the tv.

"I wasn't supposed to fall for you, Hailey, it wasn't in the plan. But apparently, the plan changed because here I am," he said nervously as he held his arms out to the side. "I don't know what any of this means, but I don't want to walk out that door and live the rest of my life wondering what could have been."

I felt a single tear roll down my cheek as I stared at this beautiful man, baring it all in front of me. Ten years I was with Glen and never once was he ever this honest with me. This was a feeling I wasn't used to and I didn't know what to do with it.

"I don't know what to say," I whispered as I folded my hands in my lap and looked down. He walked over and kneeled in front of me, placing his hands on top of mine.

"Say that you'll give me another chance. Please," he begged.

"It's too hard, all of this is too hard. You don't even know me," I countered.

"I know everything I need to know to make me want to make this work."

I took a deep breath. If he was going to be open and honest with me then I owed it to him to do the same. There was no way that we could start a relationship without having a clean slate. At least this way he could decide whether he wanted a relationship after he found out about my past.

"Do you want to know the real reason why I couldn't write those sex scenes?" I arched my eyebrow. He nodded slowly as he got up and came to sit beside me again. I turned slightly to look at him, nausea starting to build.

"I couldn't write the sex scenes because every time I tried, I would picture my ex-fiancé fucking another girl a few days after he left me at the altar. No matter how hard I tried, I couldn't get those images out of my head."

His eyes got big as I dropped the bomb in his lap. Now was the moment that he would bolt and never look back. I held my breath and waited, but instead, he shook his head sympathetically and offered a sad smile.

"I'm sorry, that really sucks. What an asshole."

"Yeah, he was, to say the least," I sighed, not wanting to get into the details about how much of an asshole he was.

"He was my first love, the only guy that I had ever been with so when he left, I was devastated. I tried a few online dating sites and had a few friends that tried to set me up, but nothing ever clicked. It was like I was dead inside."

I shifted against the couch, pulling the pillow up closer to my chest as a barrier.

"Then I met you, and immediately I was drawn to you. Listening to you through the wall was the most daring thing I had ever done, and it made me feel alive. Then we started hanging out and I found that you made me feel alive every time we were together. There was this spark there that had been missing for so long I didn't even know it existed."

He smiled as he listened, letting me talk without being interrupted.

"I know that I freaked you out with what I wrote. Honestly, I freaked myself out. My relationship with my ex ended six months ago so it felt unreal that I could already feel like I had moved on. And you weren't supposed to see it," I laughed. "That was supposed to stay a secret while I figured out what everything really meant."

"I'm glad I found out the way I did, I don't know that you would have told me otherwise," he said softly.

"Maybe not. Who knows? But it doesn't matter because you don't want a relationship, and you live in Austin now. Everything is just too hard." I threw my hands up in the air, listening to myself as I admitted out loud that there wasn't a way for us to be together. It just wasn't meant to be.

"Hailey, do you want to be with me?" He reached a finger across and gently lifted my chin to look at me.

"It doesn't matter what I want." I looked deep into his eyes, my heart breaking again inside.

"I'm going to ask again— do you want to be with me?"

"Yes," I whispered.

"Then that's all that matters," he said as he reached over and grabbed my wrists, pulling me on top of him.

"Just so we're clear, I want to be with you too." He looked up at me and smiled a smile that warmed me from the inside out.

"Now we need to talk about these pajamas," he growled as he leaned forward and nipped at my earlobe. I wrapped my arms around his neck and let my fingers play in his hair, giving it that mussed look that I loved on him.

"What's wrong with my pajamas?" I giggled as he nuzzled his nose into the crook of my neck.

"Given that the fabric is thin and you're not wearing a fucking bra, I've been sitting here with blue balls all morning and I plan to do something about it."

"Is that a threat or a promise?" I asked as his hands ran up my sides and lifted the shirt over my head before tossing it on the coffee table behind me. I sighed heavily as he leaned back and stared at me, my breasts on full display as his erection hardened beneath me.

"I don't make promises I can't deliver on, sweetheart." He pulled me down onto the couch as his hands roamed my body while his tongue worked its magic on my nipples. I thought back to the words I had written just a few days ago and realized just how wrong I was about him. He was someone who would promise me the world and would go to the ends of the earth to make sure he delivered.

<u>Epilogue</u>
3 Months Later

I set my suitcase by the door and checked my watch. I still had an hour before I needed to leave for the airport to make my flight to Austin. We had been rotating every other week with who would go where, and I was starting to get tired from traveling so much. I had to remind myself that this was what I signed up for and that real sex was better than phone sex.

I was about to go sit on the couch when there was a knock on the door. I wasn't expecting anyone and hadn't ordered delivery, so I made my way over to see who it was. As I opened the door there was a huge bouquet of red roses blocking the face of the person delivering them. I giggled as they extended both hands toward me, offering me the heavy crystal vase overflowing with fragrant roses. I took the vase and quickly smelled the bouquet as I set it on the counter, turning around to sign for them when I saw Jax instead of a delivery person.

"What are you doing here?!" I exclaimed as I brought a hand to my heart and ran over to hug him. "You're supposed to be in Austin and I'm supposed to be on a plane to come see you in an hour."

He smiled as he pressed a kiss to my lips, wrapping his arms around me as he closed the door with his foot.

"Turns out there was a change in plans," he said as he pulled back and looked at me while keeping his arms locked around my waist.

"Yeah, I'd say this was a change," I giggled still not believing that he was there in my apartment. "So, what changed?"

"It's all in the card," he said, nodding to where the flowers were.

"The card?" I pulled my eyebrows together as I felt his arms drop as he pointed to where they were sitting on the counter. I walked over and stood on my tiptoes as I peeked inside, looking for a card. Hiding in the middle of the massive bouquet was a white envelope with my name on it. I looked at him suspiciously as I pulled it out and opened it.

I slid the card out and giggled when I saw a cartoon girl sitting beneath a tree, drinking coffee, while birds lined the branches above her and a few bees were flying to the flowers beside her. The colors were bright and vibrant, reminding me of the illustrations you'd see in a children's book.

There was no writing on the front so I quickly opened it and felt my face drop when I saw that the inside was blank as well. I looked back at him as he slowly walked toward me.

"It's a beautiful card," I whispered as he wrapped his arms around my waist from behind. "But there are no words inside."

"That's because our story is still being written," he explained. "I wanted to go back to where it all started, with the birds and the bees."

I laughed as I shook my head against his chest, remembering our first real conversation together. That was in fact what had started everything between us.

"The good old birds and bees," I sighed.

"I know that I don't have the apartment next door anymore, but I was thinking maybe we could find a place together?"

His voice was low in my ear and I waited for him to go on, to ask me to leave everything here and move to Austin with him. We both knew that this was getting too hard with all of the back and forth travel but we could never bring ourselves to talk about who would be the one to give up everything and move to make the other happy. I swallowed hard, waiting for the shoe to drop. The roses and the card were just to help lighten the blow when he asked.

"Yeah?" I said wearily.

"Yeah. I was thinking that this apartment might not be big enough once we buy furniture. Maybe we should look at a house instead?"

I whipped around to look at him, a puzzled look on my face.

"You want to buy a house here when you still live in Austin? I don't think that's the best idea." I started putting numbers together in my head and immediately felt overwhelmed with the thought of trying to pay a mortgage on my own compared to the rent I was already paying which was much cheaper.

"There's no way that I can afford a mortgage, not unless I took another job and—" His finger gently reached out and pressed against my lips, shushing me.

"Hailey, I think we should buy a house together now that I'm permanently living in Arizona," he said with a smile.

"What? Since when?!"

"Since I got the promotion this morning. Turns out that my boss wants to do a lot more building out here and it just made sense for me to manage the team out here instead of going back and forth all the time."

"So you're going to be here for good? I don't have to go to Austin anymore?" I couldn't believe what I was hearing. Excitement flooded through me as I made a mental note to call and cancel my flight before it was too late. The back and forth travel had really started to add up and I didn't want to waste money on a flight I wasn't going to be on after all.

"You don't have to go to Austin anymore. And if you're okay with it, we can have one of the brand new houses they're building when it's ready. Might be a few months, but maybe we can live together here until then?"

"I can't believe this, this is amazing!" The smile stretched tight across my face as he picked me up and spun me in his arms.

"So does that mean you'll let me live with you while they build us the house of our dreams?" he teased playfully.

"Only on one condition," I said, trying to be serious.

"Okay, lay it on me," he replied as he sat me down and met my serious look with one of his own.

"You have to make me breakfast wearing those shorts that make your ass look amazing, but you don't get to wear a shirt because I like looking at all this." I reached over and ran my hands up his washboard abs and over his chest.

"Deal, but you have to promise that you won't wear anything but those sexy pajamas." He smirked as he winked.

"What about when I have to wash them?"

"Then I guess you'll just have to be naked." He shrugged his shoulders as if there weren't any other options.

"Deal," I giggled as I fell into his arms and hugged the man who made me whole again.

Acknowledgments

This book was so much fun to write, it's almost hard to believe that I wrote it in 10 days! I loved writing Hailey and Jax's story and how easily it came to me. Hailey was so relatable with her awkward interactions; I saw a lot of myself in her which might be why she spoke so clearly to me. Jax was probably one of the sexiest, dirty talking, good looking characters that I've written and will always hold a special place in my heart.

Thank you to my wonderful alpha readers for reading the first draft of this and reassuring me that I could be funny and flirty without having to kill anyone. Azucena and Chelsea, you ladies are always there when I need you and never let me down. Thank you for your constant support. I could not imagine doing any of this without you ladies.

Amanda, thank you so much for jumping into this romantic comedy! I'm still giggling over your notes and look back at them when I need something to put a smile on my face. Thank you so much for helping me with the blurb and for all of your feedback on the book. I can't wait to read your books, they're going to be so great!!

Tillie, thank you for helping with edits on this one, it means the world to me! I love your enthusiasm and excitement to read my books.

Richard, I bet you never expected to get so many written thank you notes as you do with all of these books I write! Thank you for continuing to be the most supportive person that I know and for always pushing me to keep working harder to reach my goals. You know my dreams better than I do sometimes and I'm so honored that they mean so much to you that you're so willing to help me make them come true. Thank you for taking the idea I had for the cover and adding the final touches to make it perfect! I love you so much and appreciate everything you do for me.

Thank you to my family for being supportive and showing excitement with each book that I write! I appreciate it.

To my girls, I will never stop believing that we are all capable of making our dreams come true if we're willing to try. Never forget that, the world is yours to conquer. Dream big and work even harder. I know you two will do amazing things!

To my readers, thank you so much for reading my book. If I'm a new to you author, thank you so much for giving me a chance! If you've read some of my other books, thank you so much! I hope you'll continue to follow me in this amazing journey and allow me to write the books that pull you in and make you fall in love.

About the Author

Samantha lives in the southwest with her husband and two small children after abandoning her childhood dream of living in a cabin in Colorado when she found that she couldn't afford to live there and was deathly allergic to the woods. When she's not writing she's usually spouting off sarcastic remarks while drinking wine out of a coffee mug to look like a functional adult while chasing down her toddlers. She enjoys spending time with her family, watching reruns of FRIENDS, and the 24/7 flow of coffee that can be found in her veins. Be sure to follow her on social media for updates on what she's working on.

You can find her here:

Facebook: https://www.facebook.com/AuthorSamanthaBaca

Instagram: https://instagram.com/author_samantha_baca

Goodreads: http://www.goodreads.com/authorsamanthabaca

Facebook Reader Group:
https://www.facebook.com/groups/2945710968775398/

Webpage: https://authorsamanthabaca.wordpress.com

Newsletter: http://eepurl.com/g0NcSj

Other Books

'Til Death Do Us Part (Haven Brook Book 1)
https://www.amazon.com/dp/B087TG2JZV

The Cradle Will Fall (Haven Brook Book 2)
https://www.amazon.com/dp/B08GBZG3HS

Five Steps Ahead (Dark Shadows Book 1)
http://www.amazon.com/dp/B08CMXGL9G

www.ingramcontent.com/pod-product-compliance
Lightning Source LLC
Chambersburg PA
CBHW031337010826
48972CB00012B/831